The Loons
and Other Stories

by

Penny E. Grey

ISBN: 978-0-9940840-2-6
Cover Art: from an original watercolour by Andy Alfoldy, Erickson, British Columbia

To all who inspired the writing of these stories.

Acknowledgements

My sincere thanks to my dear friend Kerry Marie Nolan for reading these stories, catching my missteps, and providing invaluable comments, on both the writing and the cover design. Her unwavering support and encouragement mean the world to me.

Contents

The Loons

Laura crouched in tall grasses at the lake's edge, rubber boots sinking slowly in black mud, camera clutched to her chest, left hand supporting the unwieldy telephoto lens. The water was like glass, and long, dark tree shadows reached over it, toward the golden-orange reflection of the setting sun. As she waited, whining night insects emerged and somewhere in the distance frogs began their night's chorus. The evening couldn't have been more perfect, the lake more beautiful.

Suddenly she saw the pair of loons she'd discovered was nesting nearby. They emerged from the grass and swam out to bask in the muted warmth of the sun's rays. She waited until they reached the tree shadows edge, then lifted the camera to her eye. They came into focus— dark, straight beaks, stark red-bead eyes, checkerboard plumage. Harmonious elegance. She snapped the picture.

...

Laura struggled to suppress an overwhelming feeling of dread as she climbed the cement steps to the school's entrance. Big double doors came into view. They were an unearthly lime green, and their bottom edges were battered from years of thumping by winter-booted toes. She stopped on the landing and looked down at her six-year-old daughter, Victoria, who was looking up at her, her small white puffs of breath rapidly forming and dissolving in the crisp January air. Straight-cut auburn bangs fell to blue-grey eyes wide with anticipation. She tightened her grip on her mother's hand. Laura turned back to the door, took a deep breath, and reached for the large, tarnished doorknob.

"I'll get it, Mom," offered nine-year-old Thomas from her other side. He grabbed the knob with two red-mittened hands and pulled.

As they stepped into the warmth of the building a smell of floor wax met Laura's nostrils. Bathed only in the light from the door, the place appeared deserted but for children painted across white cindercrete blocks on the wall at their left, skipping happily hand in hand. Tiny orange lockers lined the hallway ahead, reflecting gleaming black-and-white-squared linoleum flooring.

Laura jumped as light suddenly flooded the place. Seconds later a voice echoed across the empty corridor. "You must be Mrs. Bailey."

An enormous woman emerged from a doorway at their right and strode toward them. Her salt-and-pepper hair was cut short, and huge black-rimmed glasses framed a round and ruddy face. The buttons of her black V-necked blouse strained to hold her heaving chest, and a voluminous skirt covered in red poinsettias reached to thick ankles. Her feet were stuffed into sensible black shoes.

"Yes," Laura replied, suddenly aware of the puddles forming on the polished floor beneath her feet, "and this is Victoria and Thomas."

"Nice to meet you Victoria, Thomas," the woman said, beaming at the children. "I'm Mrs. Wright. I'm the principal here at St. Andrew's." She bent forward and Victoria shrank into her mother's side. Thomas's mouth fell open as the woman's huge cleavage came into view. "Why don't I show you the school before I take you to your classrooms," she said to the children, "and I'll introduce you to your teachers."

No reply.

"I think that's a very good idea, Mrs. Wright," Laura offered, mustering as much enthusiasm as she could. Mrs. Wright turned and headed down the hall ahead of them.

The principal led them down hallways and into classrooms, through library and gymnasium, her voice booming in the empty spaces as she proudly described the new science lab, the recent acquisition of computers, the rousing success of the school's athletes at the fall indoor track meet. Laura tried to concentrate, but her apprehension only grew as they walked. She glanced up at a white-faced clock, its large black hands pointing to eight thirty. The other children would be coming in soon—greeting familiar faces, finding familiar classrooms, continuing familiar lessons— and she would have to leave Victoria and Thomas among them, unfamiliar with it all. She listened to the soles of their boots squeaking on the lino and watched the red poinsettias sway rhythmically on the checkerboard floor.

...

It was almost dark. Laura rose from her crouched position and winced as her knee joints popped. Pulling her boots from the sucking mud, she retreated to the forest's edge. As the sun dipped beneath the trees, a three-quarter moon cast a blue light on the lake. She spotted the loons—two ghosts gliding effortlessly through the water, leaving gentle ripples in their wake.

She retraced her steps along the shore, absorbing the smells of pine needles and timber floating on the warm damp air. She walked slowly, not wanting the bliss of her evening to end.

As she neared home she could see light coming from the living room, glowing softly through the trees. Just then the loons began calling from the lake.

A hauntingly beautiful and lonely cry.

...

"And this is Thomas's classroom."

Laura followed Mrs. Wright into a spacious yellow room, Victoria in tow. Thomas's new teacher was waiting inside, tiny and blond and pretty, and she greeted him warmly and offered to show him around the room. He followed her reluctantly, looking nervously back at his mom. Laura smiled encouragingly, her eye caught by the wall beyond. It was almost obscured by poster-size paintings in primary colours. A large table stood at the back of the room, sporting what appeared to be volcanoes in various stages of completion, and five rows of six desks occupied the centre space. Thirty students, thought Laura.

A far cry from the thirteen classmates Thomas had at his previous school. She watched him approach the far corner of the room. Something in a cage stirred and he leaned toward it.

"Shall we move on to Victoria's room?" asked Mrs. Wright.

Laura nodded and called out to her son: "I'm going with Victoria now, Thomas, okay?"

Thomas whirled around and looked at her, panicked, his face chalk white against his dark hair. For a split second he wavered, then caught himself. He looked down at the floor. "Okay, Mom," he murmured, and he turned solemnly back to the cage.

Laura swallowed hard. His first day ever at school flashed before her—the fear in his dark eyes, the tears. She had to leave him crying then, but she knew he wouldn't cry now. Though he was still a little boy, he wouldn't risk looking like one for anything in the world. That's just what it was to be eight.

...

"You're home a day early," Laura said to her husband, Daniel, as she closed the door behind her. The room smelled of cedar and was warm from the heat of a fire blazing in the fireplace.

"Yes, there was no point in staying the extra day."

She looked at him. He looked tired. His unruly sandy-brown hair fell across his forehead, and his blue shirt, rumpled and rolled at the sleeves, was open at the collar, his tie loosened and lying askew. "Where are the kids?" he asked.

"They're at the Hansen's for the night. They were dying to go, and I thought it would be a great opportunity to get some pictures."

Pale-green eyes looked into hers. "I got the offer."

She hesitated a split second. "Oh . . . well . . . that's good news," she said quietly, turning to look out the big picture window to the lake. She saw only her own reflection.

"It's a great offer," Daniel went on. "And the city's nice, not too big." He paused. "The school looks great." He moved toward her and his voice softened. "You'll like it, hon. I'm *sure* you will." He stood behind her and placed large roughened hands on her shoulders, squeezing gently. "It's a good move for us, Laura."

Laura turned and looked into his handsome face, tanned from years in the outdoors. "I know."

...

Mrs. Wright led the way back down the hall. Though Victoria's hand still held hers, Laura was less worried about her daughter. Victoria had been beside herself with excitement on her first day of school only three short months ago. She couldn't wait to get there, and she didn't notice when her mother left.

The poinsettia skirt turned into one of the recessed doorways at the end of the corridor. Inside the baby-blue room stood Victoria's new teacher, smiling and spectacled. Her face was soft and round and wrinkled, like an overripe peach, and framed in the stern black-and-white habit of a Catholic nun. A decades-old smell of starch and talcum powder suddenly swept into Laura's nose as she remembered fondly her own grade-one teacher. Then an ear-splitting scream shattered the memory and Victoria, her face white with fear, burst into heart-rending sobs and threw herself into her mother's arms.

In a few minutes, Laura managed to calm her daughter, and when the Sister showed Victoria the huge rosary hidden in a secret pocket in her skirt, a faint smile appeared on her daughter's tear-stained face. With a final shuddering sigh, she took the nun's hand and walked toward tiny desks arranged in a circle in the middle of the room. Laura looked wearily at Mrs. Wright, who smiled sympathetically. "Don't worry," the principal said. "She'll be all right." Victoria was already settled in her desk, watching the Sister's face, a little in awe, as she spoke.

Laura reached the lime-green doors just as the other children were coming in—noisy, happy, and breathless with hard play. She reached her car, brushing away a tear threatening to spill over. She turned and headed back to the new house.

...

Laura shivered in relief as the first rays of the sun reached her, crouching again in the lake grasses, and carefully wiped the lens once more, afraid that the morning mist would ruin her chances. It had been several weeks since she had found the nest with its treasure of two perfect eggs, and she waited patiently, some distance away, for the young family to emerge.

Just as she was beginning to lose the feeling in her toes, she heard a rustling, and then the tips of the grasses stirred as the loons made their way through to the open water. She lifted the camera and looked for two chicks, but there was only one, nestled safely on mom's back. Her heart sank. The water birds living on the lake were easy prey for foxes, but she'd hoped these loons would escape notice. She rose stiffly and slopped through the mud toward the nest. Tiny pieces of shell lying several feet away were the evidence that nature's cruel hand had been played.

She turned and watched the loons swim away from her, mom with chick, then dad. Somehow she knew they wouldn't be back. There was an urgency in their morning swim; they were moving to a safer place, a better place. She raised her camera once more and focused on the chick, bathed by the sun in a golden aura of down.

And took the shot.

...

Laura was on her knees on the living room carpet, stuffing paper back into empty boxes, when she noticed a large picture box hiding behind the couch. She crawled over to it and pulled it toward her, then swept a long strand of hair from her face and lifted the wrapped frame from its box. She slowly tore away the tissue paper covering it and gazed lovingly at the photograph of the loons, all the sights and smells and sounds of the lake rushing back to her.

Suddenly she remembered Victoria and

Thomas. She looked at her watch—she should have been there fifteen minutes ago! But just as she scrambled up from the floor, she heard the back door open and a voice calling, "Mom!" It was Victoria.

"Victoria!" Laura called back, a little alarmed, as she made her way through mountains of paper to the kitchen. "How did you get home?" The little girl looked up at her, a smile reaching from ear to ear, her eyes bright with excitement. "Jennifer knows the way," she said matter-of-factly.

"Jennifer? Who's Jennifer?"

"My friend, Jennifer," Victoria replied, as if surprised her mother didn't know her, and she pointed to a green parka coming in behind her. Laura could just make out a tiny pair of glasses and black bangs under the hood. "Can Jennifer come in to play, Mom?" her daughter asked as both girls removed their snow-encrusted boots.

A smile teased the corners of Laura's mouth as she watched the girls shed their coats. "Sure she can." A great weight had lifted from her shoulders. "But where's Thomas?"

"He's over in the park with my brother," Jennifer informed her. "Across the street."

"He'll be home in a while," added Victoria.

Laura smiled again. "He will, will he?" She watched the two little girls, hair waving with static electricity, wade through the lake of paper, making swimming motions and giggling. She laughed as they disappeared around the corner. Then she heard a frightened squeal and hurried toward it. As she rounded the corner she spotted the huge, staring face of the bearskin rug emerging from the corner of a cardboard box, then heard Victoria's voice, explaining.

"That's Bear," she was saying. "He's from the lake."

Shadows

On the first day of the new semester, Ellen woke with a start, heart racing and brain whining at the abrupt transition from deep sleep. She lay on her back, arms rigid at her sides, legs pressed together, willing her eyes to see the familiar corners of her bedroom, struggling to erase the horrifying images and sounds of her nightmare.

But she could see nothing in the winter-darkened room, save a patch of wall beyond the foot of the bed, dimly striped by streetlight passing through venetian blinds. She focused her mind's eye instead, tracing delicate petals of tiny yellow flower clusters on the wallpaper, then green leaves, slowly replacing the blood-spattered scene in her head with diminutive bouquets tied with blue ribbons. Gradually the real in her world replaced the unreal, though the terror lingered at the edges of her consciousness, a hungry animal ready to pounce if she let down her guard.

She drew a deep breath and let it out slowly, her body sinking into the mattress. Her heart slowed to normal and her brain quieted. The nightmare was gone, but she didn't dare let her eyes close again. She raised herself onto her right elbow and looked at the glowing red numbers of the clock radio on her bedside table: 4 a.m. She groaned. It was going to be a *very* long day. She rolled back onto the pillow and shivered, despite flannel pajamas and a mountain of bedcovers up to her nose.

Her eyes went back to the wall, and suddenly a tingling started in her scalp and moved in a prickly wave to her toes. The striped patch was changing shape. Something was casting a shadow. Something growing. She was unable to move, unable to wrest her eyes from it, unwilling to lose her hold on what little light she had to see anything at all.

But then the shadow changed and took on a familiar shape: two pointed ears, a long nose. She giggled involuntarily, stuck her hand out into the frigid air, and jumped when the cold, wet nose of her German shepherd found her.

"Hey there, Tobias," she said, kneading the dog's big head in the darkness. "How're ya doin'?" Tobias yawned noisily and rested his chin on the bed. "I know. It *is* too early to get up. How 'bout some company?" She patted the top of the bed, and the dog jumped up and lay beside her. Comforted by his presence, she gently rubbed his warm belly, wondering how she had forgotten her loyal companion lying there in his bed on the floor, as he did every night. For a moment she had thought the grotesque black figure in her nightmare was back. But it was not real. She knew that.

That's what she got for finishing *Dreamcatcher* the night before. She usually avoided Stephen King's books so close to bedtime, but she wanted to clear her mind of her class lectures the next day, maybe avert her usual first-day jitters. "Well, it worked, Stephen," she said aloud. "I'll be too tired today to be nervous!" Tobias thumped his tail on the bed in response to her voice.

She was avoiding the truth. It had nothing to do with the book. The nightmares she had after she left Greg had not entirely gone away, even a year later. The damage was too deep.

...

At 8 a.m. Ellen stood in the stairwell of the social sciences building, gripping the white railing, breathing hard, and looking down the seven flights she had just climbed, reconsidering the madness of her New Year's resolution. "What was I thinking?" she muttered as she stood a minute to regain her breath. She looked up the staircase, which continued for many more floors, and thanked whoever was responsible she had to go no farther.

As she neared her office midway down the hall, she noted with some pride the letters of her name incised on the black nameplate on her door: Ellen MacKinnon, Ph.D. The interview process had been merciless, but she now proudly counted herself among the faculty of the Department of Psychology. Her first term had gone very well. Her many years as a student had shown her what *not* to do as a teacher, and her years in private practice had given her knowledge that gave her additional credibility with her own students. She set her briefcase on the floor and rummaged in her coat pocket for her keys.

A voice behind her made her jump. She turned to find a man standing just a metre away. He was taller than her by several centimetres, slim in build, and she guessed in his early thirties, older than most students at the university. A shock of straight, sandy-brown hair lay across his forehead, and rectangular, metal-frame glasses sat on an unremarkable nose in a plain face. He was neatly dressed in tan corduroys and turtleneck sweater and carried a yellow ski jacket over his left arm, a black backpack over his shoulder.

"Dr. MacKinnon?" he asked.

"Yes," she replied.

He stepped toward her, hand out to shake hers. "I am in your Psychology 101 class. My name is Peter Baransky."

She smiled and took his hand. "It's nice to meet you." There was no smile in return. "Can I help you with something?"

"I wanted to introduce myself and tell you I am looking forward to your class."

His English was pretty good, but there was a significant accent, she thought maybe Slavic.

"Thank you. I hope you'll find it interesting."

"I know I will."

She started to turn back to the door but Mr. Baransky remained where he was. "Was there something else?" she asked.

He hesitated a split second. "I want to know if I could come and talk to you sometime." His eyelids drooped a little, like a hound's.

"Of course. My students are welcome to come to my office if they have questions."

"Thank you," he said without expression. He turned and walked quietly down the hall.

She watched as he disappeared around the corner. *A bit odd,* she thought.

She stepped into her office. The window covering most of the wall opposite the door framed only dull grey light. Shelves lined the wall to her left, most of them filled with books standing straight as soldiers, some with papers in neat piles. Her antique desk—clean but for blotter, computer components, and desk lamp—sat in front of the window, facing the door. Her smaller animal skulls—she'd had to leave the larger ones in her collection at home for lack of space here—grinned at her from behind glass doors in a cabinet on the right. Two chairs in front sat on a Persian rug in rusts and browns. During the Christmas break she had replaced the university's furniture with her own, and she was pleased with the result. It now had a professional yet welcoming look.

She emptied her briefcase and got down to work at her desk, organizing her tasks for the week, preparing for her morning class. When she entered the lecture hall at 10 a.m., she was greeted by upwards of two hundred students, some appearing eager, others reserved, some very young, others older; row upon row of them rose upward from her position on the floor. Though she looked for him, it was impossible to spot her early-morning visitor in the sea of faces. As the last few students trickled in and found seats, she dimmed the lights and attached the microphone to her suit jacket. Hundreds of laptops opened en masse and fingers poised themselves above keys. She began: "Good morning and welcome to Psychology 101."

...

Back in her office an hour later, Ellen settled herself at her desk and prepared materials for the department meeting later in the week. She was starting to feel the loss of sleep early this morning, but the time passed quickly. After eating her bag lunch at her desk, she took a brisk walk outdoors, clearing her head, refreshing herself in the crisp winter air. Soon she was gathering her books and papers together in her office for her 3 p.m. class. Just as she pulled her door shut she heard a voice: "Hello, Dr. MacKinnon."

"Oh, hello again, Mr. . . . ." she looked once more into an impassive face.

"Baransky. Please call me Peter."

"Something I can help you with, Peter?"

"Yes. I want to know if I could talk to you."

She looked at her watch. "I'm just on my way to class."

"I will walk with you."

She looked at him, hesitant for a second. "Fine. I'm going down to the main floor."

She started down the hall, Mr. Baransky silent beside her. She headed toward the stairs, then thought better of it and turned to the elevator. "What is it you want to talk to me about, Peter?" she asked as she pushed the elevator button.

"I bought the textbook for your class at the bookstore." A loud *bing* announced the elevator's arrival and they stepped inside.

"Yes?"

"I notice there is a lot of science in it."

"Yes, there is *some*. I indicated that in class this morning." She watched the numbers above the elevator doors light up in turn as they descended.

"I have no knowledge of science. I will need help."

"You needn't worry, Peter," she said as the doors opened onto the main floor and they stepped out. "It's an introductory course. I'm sure there are others like you who have no science background." She continued down the hall, Mr. Baransky a shadow beside her.

"I will do my best," he said.

"Good. I hope all my students have your attitude." She stopped. "This is my room. See you in our next class." She turned toward the door, then stopped again as his voice pursued her.

"So, could I come and talk to you sometime?"

She looked at the stone face, the dead eyes, and felt a crease form in her forehead. "Yes, Peter," she said a little slowly, "that would be fine."

"Thank you." He turned and walked back the way they had come, his nose pointed at the floor.

More than a bit odd.

...

The next morning Ellen stood on the landing of the seventh-floor stairwell, right hand on the door handle, staring through the glass window in disbelief at the back of a yellow ski jacket and black backpack at her office door. "What is *with* this guy?" she muttered, unease playing with her spine like a cat with a new toy. She paused for a few seconds, mustering up her best authoritative-professor demeanor, then gripped her briefcase, pulled open the door, and strode down the hall.

"Good morning, Peter," she said as brightly as she could. He wheeled around as if startled from concentrated thought. "What can I do for you?"

"I want to know if I could come and talk to you today."

Her grip on her briefcase tightened. "Of course, Peter, but the class has hardly begun."

"I was reading the textbook last night and I have a few questions."

"Oh, okay, you can drop by during my office hours this afternoon." She unlocked her office door.

"What time should I come?"

She stared at the door a few seconds, then turned slowly and directed his attention to the student appointment sign-up sheet hanging next to her door. "Any time between one and three o'clock would be fine, Peter. As you can see, I'm not expecting anyone else today."

He nodded and she continued into her office, closed the door, and hung up her coat. Her skin was crawling, and she rubbed her arms vigorously, wanting to feel any sensation other than the one causing her neck hairs to stand up. She went to her chair and opened her lecture notes for her morning class, hoping to distract herself. She raised her head to a light knocking at her door. Before she could respond, it opened. Mr. Baransky stood holding the doorknob, one foot inside her office. "I want to tell you that I will come at two o'clock," he said.

She replied with considerable effort: "Two o'clock, then." He stepped back and closed the door, and the pencil in her hand snapped in two.

She knew she was being ridiculous. Peter Baransky was different, yes, but his level of formality, strange to almost anyone in this country, was likely rooted in cultural differences. He appeared needy, but if he'd ventured alone to a university far from his own country, he was probably lonely, a little desperate for human contact.

No, Mr. Baransky was not the problem. Her problem was she was still getting over Greg. She was oversensitive to any man trying to move into her space, mental *or* physical, and Mr. Baransky was definitely pushing her boundaries. She was all too familiar with the knots now tightening in her stomach. For ten years her husband had barely let her breathe. She shivered and sat back in her chair.

How could she have let it happen? She was a

graduate student in *psychology* when she met Greg. She should have recognized the type, his need to control everything. Every*thing* and every*body*. But no, she was dazzled instead. He exuded charm from every pore and he wined and dined her, waited on her hand and foot. She liked to think she was just too focused on her studies at the time to be aware, but in truth she was simply rendered blind by the attention. The day she held her Ph.D. degree in her hands, he presented an engagement ring to her—a solid-gold band with three diamonds embedded in it—and she didn't even hesitate to say yes.

She shook her head in disbelief. All the red flags had been there, but she hadn't seen them. She was so excited about getting her practice up and running that she was delighted when Greg offered to handle the wedding plans. And then he chose the neighbourhood they would live in and did the house hunting himself. Each time he made a decision for them she found the positive in it. She could focus on her work and didn't have to worry about a thing at home. She thought she'd died and gone to heaven.

But Greg was a master at control. Like a tiger walking quietly through tall grasses, he knew how to camouflage his intent, but in the end he always got what he was after. And she was easy prey. After all, she was happy to vacation in Maui instead of Greece; and it was nice to spend a Saturday night just the two of them, instead of with friends; and she did enjoy working out at a gym instead of running in the neighbourhood.

On the surface she had a great life: a beautiful home, a fulfilling career, and a doting husband. But in time she lost her love of cooking for fear of Greg's criticism about the meal, and she dressed in the bathroom to avoid his advice about what she should wear. It was years before she noticed that she was carefully considering everything she wanted to say to him, and how to say it, before speaking, often not saying anything at all rather than have it dismissed. Eventually she became Pavlov's dog, automatically responding as he wished, unable to do anything else.

She had only one escape from him: her work. At her office she was the strong, independent woman she had been before she met Greg. Just being in her own space, and without him, made all the difference. She didn't quite understand it. How could she feel completely out of control at home and completely in charge at the office?

But she'd met enough women, some men too, in her practice to know that there were all kinds of abuse, and they all seemed to work the same way: consistent and persistent reinforcement and punishment. She had seen women in her office who couldn't even look her in the eye after decades with power-hungry and often violent spouses. And as the years passed she came to realize that she was becoming one of them.

...

It was 2 p.m. exactly when Ellen heard a light rapping on her office door. She was on the phone, talking to her answering machine at home, purposely making Mr. Baransky wait, taking control of the meeting from the outset.

But he *didn't* wait. She still had the phone to her ear when he simply opened the door and walked in. He closed the door and sat down in one of the chairs opposite her, placing his backpack and jacket on the other.

She told her machine she'd call back later, and hung up the phone. "Peter," she said, "I was on the phone. Please don't walk into my office without invitation."

"But you were expecting me at two o'clock," he replied, then looked at his watch. "It is now a minute *past* two o'clock."

Something had changed in his manner. He was no longer the quiet, passive man she had spoken with in the hallway. Her shoulders tightened. "My students wait outside until I'm ready to receive them, Peter."

"I am not just your student, Dr. MacKinnon," he said. "I am your friend."

She could feel goosebumps emerge on her arms, underneath the long sleeves of her white blouse. "My friend?"

"We have spoken many times already and you said I could come and talk to you." His eyes looked, unblinking, into hers.

"About the psychology course, yes, but—"

"I want us to be friends."

She stared at him, stunned. "That's not appropriate, Peter. I'm your professor. We can't be friends."

"If you were *not* my professor, what then?"

The artery in her temple was throbbing. "I don't want you to drop my psychology class, Peter."

"Our friendship is more important to me than your psychology class."

She responded slowly, carefully: "Mr.

Baransky, you are my student. Nothing more." She opened the textbook in front of her. "Now, let's get to your questions."

But Mr. Baransky did not respond as she'd hoped. He rose from his chair and gathered up his jacket and backpack. "For now, I am your student, Dr. MacKinnon," he said, "But I know in time you will feel differently."

And then he left her office, closing the door quietly behind him.

She stared at the door, unable to believe what had just transpired. Despite her preparation, he had controlled the entire conversation, short as it was. She went over and over what she had said, what *he* had said. She couldn't have done anything differently—he had not allowed it—and somehow the situation had gotten even worse.

Her heart pummelled her rib cage. She got up from her chair and circled her office, taking deep breaths to calm herself. She considered talking to her department head, as Mr. Baransky's language could be construed as sexual harassment, but she quickly dismissed the idea. He had spoken only of friendship and, as inappropriate as it might be, a third party may not see enough in it to act upon.

She knew she could also be overreacting. She

had worked hard on her mental recovery over the past year, but her experience with clients had shown her that it can take a very long time to heal. She definitely didn't want her department head to think she was unable to cope. Besides, the department head would likely suggest first that she be very clear to the student about boundaries. She had made it as plain as she could to Mr. Baransky that their relationship was one of professor and student only, but she would explain more thoroughly about the university's rules next time.

She stood in front of her office window and looked out. The bare limbs of trees below her clawed the sky as the wind buffeted them, and walkers skirted the snow drifting across their path as they scurried between buildings. She shivered as a shadow fell over all when the low winter sun disappeared behind a dark cloud.

...

At home that evening, Ellen sat cross-legged on the rug in the middle of the floor of her upstairs study, documents organized in piles around her, her thoughts on the research paper she'd started before Christmas. Tobias lay flat on his side against the wall, his paws occasionally twitching in his sleep.

So concentrated was she on her work that she jumped when the phone rang. She rose awkwardly from the floor, trying not to topple her paper piles, her feet tingling as blood returned to them. She walked to the other side of the table that served as her home desk space.

"Hello?"

"Hello, Dr. MacKinnon?"

She clambered for the receiver as it slipped from her hand, catching it before it hit the desk, and raised it back to her ear. "Mr. Baransky," she said, feigning calm, her heart racing. "How did you get my home phone number?"

"I found it online."

She sat down hard in the chair. She never listed her home phone number anywhere, not since Greg. She took a deep breath. "Please don't call me at home, Mr. Baransky."

"I want to ask you a few questions—"

"Not at home. If you have questions, see me in my office during my office hours." She quickly hung up. She stared at the telephone for an eternity, expecting it to ring again, but it didn't. She put her elbows on the desk and her head in her hands. She shook all over. Tobias got up and walked to her, slipped his head under her arm, and rested it in her lap.

It was Greg all over again.

A year ago she had started going to a fellow psychologist, a colleague down the hall from her own practice. She knew they had to first understand why Greg had so easily taken control of her, but her goal was to work with her colleague on strategies to help Greg with his control issues while at the same time rebuild her own confidence and independence. She knew the marriage would benefit from bringing better balance to *both* of them.

But she'd only had two appointments when fate intervened.

One morning she heard her secretary on the phone just outside her office door, relaying her day's schedule to someone. Her jaw dropped in disbelief. It could only be Greg.

"Marjorie, what are you *doing?*" she said, causing the girl to jump in her seat. Marjorie quickly hung up the phone and turned her seat to face her employer.

"Oh . . . hi, Dr. MacKinnon. That was Gr—Mr. MacKinnon. I . . . thought you were with a client."

"The client cancelled." She struggled to keep

from raising her voice. "You were telling my husband my *client schedule,* Marjorie?"

"He just wants to be sure you're not overworking, Dr. MacKinnon," Marjorie responded.

She was stupefied. "Marjorie, what goes on in this office stays in this office. Client privilege is the most important thing here. I thought I made that very clear to you. How long has this been going on?"

"Since I started working here, but—"

"What!" Ellen's throat suddenly went dry, threatening to choke her. Marjorie had been with her for five years. Her mind flew back to the years before that, when she answered her own phone. She suddenly realized Greg's daily calls *then* were nothing about showing his affection for her. He was checking up.

Marjorie folded her arms on her chest. "But I didn't tell him client *names,* just *when* you had clients."

"Nevertheless, my schedule is none of his business!" And then she saw something suddenly change in Marjorie's eyes. Instead of respect, defiance. Greg had gotten to her.

"Greg didn't want you to think he was being

foolish," said Marjorie. "He's crazy in love with you, you know. He said so." And then she turned away from her employer and went back to her computer.

Ellen could think of nothing else to say. None of this was Marjorie's fault. She knew too well Greg's charm. But he had gone too far. Her practice was hers and hers alone—the only thing she had left she could say that about—and he was not going to take it from her. She was a mother bear protecting her cub from an intruder—enraged.

...

The morning after her disturbing phone call in her home study, Ellen pulled into the faculty parking lot and turned automatically into her usual spot. She gasped and suddenly slammed on the brakes to avoid Peter Baransky, who was standing in her parking space. The back end of her car slid sideways on the ice and narrowly missed the neighbouring vehicle. She watched him step aside and then straightened her car and nudged it the rest of the way in. She sat where she was for several seconds, her gloved hands fluttering in her lap, waiting for her pulse to return to normal. The door opened beside her.

"I am sorry, Dr. MacKinnon. I did not mean to startle you."

She stepped out of the car. "Mr. Baransky, what are you doing here? How did you know where I park?"

"You do not have office hours today, and I want to ask you some questions." He adjusted his backpack on his shoulder. "I will walk with you."

"I won't talk to you now, Mr. Baransky. Office hours only." She turned away from him and headed for the social sciences building, walking briskly. She didn't know if he was following her, but dared not look back to check. Once inside she walked directly to the ladies' room just down the hall on the main floor and stood staring at her ghost-pale face in the mirror. She clung to the counter, trying to keep her shaking knees from spilling her onto the floor.

Ten minutes later she had composed herself as best she could and started the climb to the seventh floor, desperately trying to convince herself she was overreacting, being ridiculous. Peter Baransky clearly had a problem with boundaries but probably wasn't even aware that what he was doing was wrong. He was clearly accustomed to getting his own way. Maybe it was a cultural thing, maybe it was his upbringing, but she was a professional and needed to act like one. She had to stop this now, explain to him that his behaviour wasn't acceptable.

But a familiar voice calling to her suddenly shattered her concentration, and she tripped on the next stair. Only her death grip on the railing saved her from crashing to her knees.

"Dr. MacKinnon?" it called again.

She looked over the railing and caught a glimpse of a black backpack several flights below. She quickened her pace. Just one more flight to go. She was breathing hard when she reached the landing of the eighth floor. *Eighth*? She wheeled around and raced down the stairs, burst through the seventh-floor door, and tried not to run down the hall. She glanced toward the stairs as she fumbled with her keys at her office door. She saw one of her graduate students, *not* Peter Baransky, come through the stairwell door, wave at her, and adjust his black backpack on his shoulder. She raised her hand in acknowledgement.

...

Tired as she had been when she got home after her encounter with her receptionist, Ellen was determined to address the issue with Greg right away. But it turned out the ball was not in her court. When she stepped into the kitchen from the garage, he was there waiting.

"I got a call from Marjorie today," he said, cool as a cucumber.

"I intend to fire Marjorie," she replied, setting her briefcase onto a kitchen chair.

"You'll do no such thing." His voice quivered a little.

"I certainly will. She can no longer be trusted."

"I'll say it again. You'll do no such thing." The muscles of his jaw bulged as he took a step toward her.

She stood her ground. "It's *my* practice, Greg, not yours. I will be getting a new receptionist and *he* will not be giving you my schedule."

"He?" he cackled. "Do you think that will make any difference?"

"You can't control *everyone*, Greg."

"I don't *need* to control everyone." A shadow crawled onto his face.

"What's *that* supposed to mean?"

"I've got *you,* don't I?" And before she had time to register it, his arm had swung out and then back again and his open palm made contact with her cheek, sending a thousand needles into her face. She fell against the granite countertop, catching the edge in her ribs, and went down onto the tile floor, the breath knocked out of her.

As she lay there gasping, dozens of faces of abused wives passed before her eyes, and she realized she was now one of them. Had always been one of them. She tried to speak, but her breath wasn't quite there yet.

"What did you say?" It was Greg.

She slowly got to her feet, her breath almost back now. "I said thank you."

"For what?"

"For helping me see things clearly."

She left Greg that night. And when she handed her wedding band to him as a sign of her determination, he simply placed it on his little finger, next to the matching band on his ring finger, and waved it in her face. His insane confidence that she would be back was written all over the maniacal grin on his face.

...

By the time Ellen's last class that afternoon was finished, she was exhausted and just wanted to get home. It was already dark outside. She welcomed the cold air and breathed deeply, wrapping her woollen scarf around her neck when the wind threatened to carry it away. She walked to her car without glancing over her shoulder, trying at least to *look* confident that Peter Baransky would not be following her. She hadn't seen him since she arrived this morning. She wondered if he'd finally gotten the message. She reached her car and climbed in, locking the doors and scanning what she could see of the area around her. She was absolutely alone. She shook her head at herself as she waited for the car to warm up. Greg was still in her head, eroding her will, chipping away her strength, crushing her independence. Until he was gone from there, she would not truly be in control, of herself or her life. She decided to call tomorrow and make an appointment to see her old colleague.

Tobias greeted her in the garage, where his doghouse kept him warm and dry. But he didn't bounce playfully around her as was his habit. He went through his dog door to the patio and, when she opened the utility door and joined him, he seemed particularly eager to get into the house. She was a little late getting home and thought he must be hungry. She unlocked the back door and he entered the house, but instead of rushing, as he usually did, to show her where he'd left his food bowl that morning, he stiffened and crouched low to the floor, stepping slowly, carefully, a predator on prey. His hackles rose and he stopped in the middle of the room, his nose toward the stairs at the other side. A barely audible growl rumbled in his throat.

Ellen lowered her briefcase to the floor and walked slowly toward her protector, a nervous energy rising inside her. She touched his neck and they started forward. When they reached the bottom of the stairs, she looked up to see a glow of light coming from her study.

She knew who it must be.

When she and Tobias reached the open door, he was sitting on the edge of the near side of the table, relaxed and seemingly at home, his face in darkness. The desk lamp next to him cast his shadow on the wall. It loomed above him and reached across the ceiling toward her. His head was down, apparently engaged by a skull in his hand. She recognized it on the wall—the wolf. He looked up at her as she entered the room. Tobias growled, low and menacing, at her side.

"How did you get in here?" she asked, deadly calm.

He put the skull on the desk behind him and

rose to his feet. "I've got a question for you," he said. His mouth continued to move, but she could no longer hear him.

She spoke.

And Tobias responded, throwing himself at the man's chest, knocking him backward over the table and down onto the floor on the other side, taking the wolf and the lamp with them. She watched the misshapen black figure on the wall, man and dog as one, legs and arms, fur and tail, in a macabre dance. It was her nightmare's image and the sound of her nightmare came from it: a dog's growling and a man's screaming, neither human nor animal, but both.

But this time she wasn't afraid.

Within seconds the black figure stopped moving and a terrible quiet settled on the room. A long nose and two pointed ears appeared on the wall and Tobias returned to where she stood. She crouched and hugged him hard, the tears streaking her cheeks, commingling with the blood of her tormentor on the dog's face.

She rose and walked to the table in search of the phone, choosing not to look at what lay sprawled on the hardwood floor behind it. She picked up the receiver and pressed 911, then moved slowly around the desk.

"Police emergency," said a voice in her ear.

But she didn't respond. She could now see what the shadow on the wall could not show her. The man's head was turned toward her, covered in blood, the cheek hanging away from its bone and revealing a ghastly grin of even teeth. But she had no trouble recognizing the man. Beyond the torn flesh of his throat and the pool of blood beneath his shoulder were the man's left arm and five long fingers reaching desperately for help.

And six diamonds on two gold bands, side by side, sparkling in the light of the fallen lamp just beyond his grasp.

Sea Mist

Lisa squeezed Will's hand with nervous anticipation as they stepped onto the weathered planks of the dock at Darnell Bay. The morning air was cool, but the sun was bright and warm on her face. The marina was quiet this early in the spring, but a light breeze rippled the water's surface. It was a perfect day for their first sail of the year. *Sea Mist* bobbed gently in her slip, beckoning them, and Lisa's heart quickened. As they got closer, she could see the water's reflection dancing on the boat's shiny white hull.

The boat looked magnificent after the winter refurbish, teak decks gleaming and chrome rails sparkling. As Lisa boarded she detected a lingering odour of varnish. It even smells new, she thought. Her excitement threatened to bubble over. She was counting on *Sea Mist*, counting on her to put the smile back onto Will's face, to put the life back into his eyes. He needed to forget what had happened and move on. She hoped a weekend on the water would do the trick.

Lisa and Will descended the few steps into the cabin. Lisa drew open the curtains, flooding the space with sunlight, and eagerly watched Will's face—a face aged ten years, it seemed, in the last few months—as he surveyed their surroundings. The blue-and-green wildflowers pattern she had chosen for the fabric of the seat cushions, the shining white countertops with just a touch of gold veining in them, the new oak cabinets. The cabinets. Will ran his hand lovingly over the wood, caressing it. Lisa sensed the pride he felt in the work he had done, the pride he had always felt before, but hadn't felt for a long time. His eyes met hers and a smile teased the corners of his mouth. *Sea Mist* was working her magic.

A short while later, checklists completed, they motored away from the dock. Lisa set herself to preparing the mainsail, pausing for a moment and closing her eyes, revelling in the salty perfume of the Pacific. She opened her eyes and gazed into a cloudless blue sky. The mouth of the bay loomed ahead, and she could see the rougher waters of Moore's Channel beyond. It was going to be a wonderful day for sailing. She turned toward Will and smiled at what she saw. His red beard was ablaze in the bright morning sun, and he wore his favourite wool turtleneck, the dark green one, under his yellow slicker. Standing there, his large hands gripping the wheel, his hair blown back by the wind, he painted a handsome picture of a captain.

Lisa returned to the task at hand, but her thoughts slipped back to that horrible week in February, when it had all started, when Will's father had died. He went in his sleep in his own bed—they were thankful for that—but it was so sudden, so unexpected, they'd had no time to prepare. The sixty-six-year-old worked alongside his two sons right up to that day, sanding and smoothing; it was all his arthritic hands would allow after forty-four years in the business. He taught Will and the younger Gary everything he knew about the wood, the tools, the art of cabinet making. And after twenty years, Sadler and Sons was renowned for their fine work across the country.

But they had been living a fairy tale.

Lisa was brought back to the present by Will's voice. "Prepare to raise the mainsail."

Lisa loosened the last of the mainsail rigging. "Ready," she said. She took his place at the helm. The sail billowed as Will raised it to the top of the mast, growing until it towered over them like a great white tent. She guided the boat out of the bay, and as the sail filled she turned off the engine. Will drew the sail into position to capture the southerly wind, and *Sea Mist* leaned gently as they made their way along the channel.

The small Dawes Island, just outside the bay, was on Lisa's left, and she sailed *Sea Mist* parallel to its shore while Will secured the mainsail rigging. She watched him make his way to the foredeck, where he unwrapped and rigged the smaller foresail. Soon the foresail rose and filled. After securing it, he took the wheel from her, and Lisa sat down to enjoy the ride. The sails obscured much of her view of Dawes, but she could clearly see the point ahead. They would probably make the turn around the island in less than an hour, and then, with the wind behind them, they would have an enjoyable sail to Carlton Island, where they would spend the night.

The death of William Sadler Sr. had been a shock for everyone. Will was particularly close to him and took it very hard. He was quiet at the funeral but he cried long and hard at home. His eyes still glistened with tears whenever he spoke of his dad. But that had only been the beginning. It was a few days later when the company's lawyer called, and the bottom dropped out of their lives.

The senior Sadler was a good man, but he lacked business sense, a fact he managed to keep from his family for twenty years. He had overextended their credit with suppliers, and the large contract they had with an East Coast client had fallen through. The books showed that *many* of their clients were in arrears or had cancelled after the work was underway, choosing instead the less expensive, machine-produced products. The family was stunned, and in the months that followed, they watched, numb with grief, as their precious wood, then their tools, then their art was taken from them.

Will's voice interrupted Lisa's thoughts once again. "We're coming up to the point. Prepare to make the turn." She eased the foresail and Will drew in the mainsail as they passed the point of the island. When they were both ready he turned *Sea Mist* away from the wind, bringing her around almost 180 degrees to head north to Carlton Island. Lisa stayed down as the boom, carrying the deadly force of the wind, passed over her head, carrying the mainsail to the opposite side.

The wind was now behind them, and they let

both sails out until they were almost perpendicular to it, one on either side of the boat. Now that they were running with the wind, it was suddenly quiet, and Lisa's face, tightened by the salty hand of the ocean, relaxed and warmed. She stood beside her husband and he slipped an arm around her waist, planting a quick kiss on her forehead. They looked up at the sails, dazzling white in the sun, and marvelled at the spectacle of it.

The wind blew steadily all afternoon, and *Sea Mist* rocked gently in the grey water as they made their way. They were not far offshore from the mainland, and they could see shore birds scurrying along the water's edge, foraging for tiny marooned sea life. Lisa was pleased to see Will relax, and her husband's mood improved as the afternoon wore on. She hadn't seen him this happy in a very long time and didn't want to disturb that, but she knew there would be no better chance to tell him something she knew he wouldn't want to hear.

"Will, I talked to Gary again this week."

"What?" He looked at her. "Lisa, we've been over this a hundred times."

"I know. But we can't go on this way."

"We're doing just fine."

"We may be doing fine, but you're miserable. You hate your job. You should be building cabinets, not installing them."

"It's a good, steady job." He paused. "There's no money in our kind of cabinet making. Nobody wants to pay for solid wood and craftsmanship anymore."

"I disagree, and so does Gary. There will always be those who want handcrafted work." Lisa looked at her husband's lined face and the grey spreading at the temples. "You've got to be happy at what you do."

Will turned to her, his dark-green eyes reflecting his tormented soul. "Even if I wanted to, there's no money." He turned away from her and gazed out over the water. Seconds passed before he said, barely audibly, "Besides, I have no head for the business end."

Lisa felt the pain in his words. He blamed himself for the bankruptcy of Sadler and Sons. "Will," she said gently, "it wasn't your fault."

Will's knuckles whitened as he tightened his grip on the wheel. "I should have been watching. I should have known what he was like." He looked up and she followed his gaze. The top of the mast swayed rhythmically, up and down, writing an indecipherable message in the sky.

Then Carlton Island appeared in the distance, and Lisa's thoughts turned toward the evening ahead. They had honeymooned there sixteen years ago, in the quaint Braidman Inn, but had never been back. They'd since explored a myriad of tiny islands on their weekend sojourns with *Sea Mist*, but never Carlton. It would be good to remember happier days.

Lisa adjusted the sails as Will turned the boat toward the island. The entrance to Sunset Bay soon appeared before them, the tops of the tall firs on either side waving and welcoming them in. As *Sea Mist* slipped into the calmer waters of the bay, Lisa dropped the foresail to the deck and began to lower the mainsail, folding and straightening the voluminous cloth and tying it in place. Will turned the engine on and motored them to the dock. It looked deserted, but they weren't surprised; it was still pretty early in the season. The small passenger ferry that serviced the islands wouldn't be running yet, not until the May long weekend, when serious preparation for the summer tourist season began.

It wasn't long before Lisa was securing *Sea*

Mist to the dock. "Let's take a walk up to the inn and see if Mrs. Braidman is open yet," she suggested. "A hot cup of her marvelous tea would be nice right now." Will agreed, and they set out on the dock to the shore. They were breathing hard when they reached the driveway that led to the inn, a long uphill climb from the water. They turned off the road and started toward the building, and their pace suddenly slowed.

They were stunned by the sight before them: sky-blue shutters in pieces on the veranda, flakes of white paint everywhere, a board nailed across the front door with a barely-legible CLOSED scrawled across it. They reached the decrepit building and Lisa put her nose up to the window in the front door. She could see the reception counter just inside, blanketed with a thick dirty layer of dust. Beyond was the staircase, the beautiful blue Persian runner she remembered now a dismal grey.

"It looks like this place has been closed for years," said Will.

Lisa turned away from the door. "What a shame," she said wistfully. "It was so beautiful."

They walked back to the main road, stopped, and took a final look. "I guess what they say is true," said Will. "You can't go back." They started back to the water, silent. Then they saw *Sea Mist* below, glowing orange in the fire of the setting sun. They quickened their pace down the hill.

Later, they lay on their backs in bed, looking up through the forward hatch, watching the stars blinking at them through the rigging. Minutes later *Sea Mist* had rocked them into a deep, troubled sleep.

...

Lisa woke early the next morning, crept out of bed, and climbed out onto the deck. The air was cold and heavy with moisture, and a thick sea mist hung like a shroud over the water. She couldn't see the shoreline. It was dead quiet save for the squeaking of the fenders as the boat bobbed in place. A shiver ran through her as she looked in the direction of the trees that sheltered the deteriorating inn. She could see nothing, and an unexplainable uneasiness stirred inside her. She returned below deck just as Will emerged, yawning, from their sleeping compartment. She turned to the tiny galley, willing away the dread she felt.

By the time they were on their second cup of coffee the first rays of the sun had cut a bright path into the cabin. Will rose and filled the sink with hot soapy water. But as Lisa began to clear the dishes from the table, a shadow stretched across the floor, darkening the cabin once again. She glanced up and saw a man silhouetted in the doorway. He was waving something menacingly at Will. She cried out and Will turned abruptly, a coffee cup flying from his soapy hands. "What the hell?"

"Get this thing goin'!" the man ordered. "We're gettin' outta here."

"Who the hell do you think you are?" Will demanded as he started up the steps. "Get the hell off my bo—"

"Now!" the man shouted, and he thrust the barrel of a handgun into Will's chest.

"Will!" Lisa cried. She seized her husband's arm and pulled him back down. "Do as he says!" She grabbed their slickers off the hook behind her and held Will's out to him. He took it from her and they climbed the stairs to the cockpit.

The mist was gone and a strong northwest wind rustled the trees and rippled the surface of the water, even in the relative protection of the bay. The sun had disappeared. Lisa felt a nauseating terror permeate her entire body. She pushed by the gunman and stepped onto the slippery dock. Her hands shook as she fumbled with the lines, and she fell to her knees, scrambling up and barely aboard as Will pulled *Sea Mist* away.

"Do you mind if I ask where we're going?" Will said coolly.

"No, I don't mind," the gunman whined sarcastically, his weapon still pointed at Will. "MacLeod Point."

MacLeod Point was northwest from Carlton Island, just over the border, in foreign waters, only a few hours' sail in decent weather. She and Will had never been there, but they'd heard of it. A filthy place with a huge harbour, where oil tankers anchored when the sea was intolerable.

Lisa looked at the gunman. He must have had a boat to be on Carlton Island at this time of year, but something must have happened to it. She could only guess how long he had been stuck on Carlton, but he looked like he hadn't eaten in a while. Greasy black hair clung to his unshaven face and steel-grey eyes stared from dark-rimmed hollows. A scrawny neck stuck out from the threadbare collar of a dingy grey plaid shirt, and an ill-fitting black leather jacket, ripped at the shoulder, hung on his narrow frame. Soiled blue jeans and badly scuffed cowboy boots completed the picture. He reeked of cigarette smoke and sweat. The terror Lisa had felt just moments before turned to disgust. MacLeod Point suited him to a T.

"In this wind it'll be a rough ride," said Will to the gunman. "We'd be better to wait—"

"Do it!"

Will glared at him, then turned resignedly to Lisa. "We'll reduce the mainsail and use the smaller foresail."

"Leave those sails down," the gunman growled. "Use the motor."

"We haven't got enough fuel to motor the whole way," Will explained impatiently. "And besides, it'll be faster if we *use* the wind rather than fight it."

The gunman looked suspiciously from Will to Lisa and then back again. "All right," he muttered, gesturing with the gun for Lisa to go ahead.

First the mainsail, then the foresail, rose over their heads, both made smaller for ease of handling the boat in the high wind. As they left the relative protection of Sunset Bay, *Sea Mist* leaned sharply, and the gunman, caught off balance, skidded across the wet floor of the cockpit and fell into the deck seat. He quickly righted himself and glared at Will, the gun at arm's length. "Warn me next time!" he snarled. His eyes were wide with rage as he moved to the opposite seat, next to Lisa.

Will looked at him impassively and leaned into the wheel. A short time later, as they reached the west side of the island, he called out to Lisa: "Prepare for the turn." Lisa nodded and gladly moved into position, repulsed by the gunman sitting so close to her. They drew in both sails, preparing to turn into the wind. She heard the breakfast dishes crashing around on the floor of the cabin as they turned, and she glanced at the gunman, now sitting above her, leaning into the wind, one hand hanging onto the rail, the other still firmly clamped to his weapon.

Sea Mist pitched heavily in the swollen waves. Lisa let the sails out to Will's specifications. I would be a slower ride but one that was easier on the boat and its passengers. As it was, it was going to be a rough and exhausting sail all the way to MacLeod Point.

The gunman turned toward Lisa. "Get me somethin' to eat."

Lisa obediently clambered to the hatch and, grabbing hold of the rails, backed cautiously down the steps. She released her hold as she stepped down to the floor of the cabin, then suddenly slammed backward into the table and fell to the floor. She had tripped on something. As she sat up, rubbing a painful elbow, she saw the black duffel bag the gunman had brought aboard, lying at the foot of the stairs. She leaned toward it and looked up into the cockpit, but no one had heard her fall.

The bag gaped open, its zipper broken. She opened it a little more. Bundles of old dirty bills—twenties, fifties, one-hundreds—jammed the bag to the brim. Then she heard an ugly voice coming from the cockpit. She grabbed a couple of sandwiches, leftovers from yesterday's lunch, and went above.

"Get ready to move to the opposite side," Will shouted at the gunman. Then he turned to Lisa and gestured to her to come and take the wheel. He looked directly, steadily, into her eyes.

She returned his gaze. She understood and nodded imperceptibly. She moved to the helm.

"Stay where you are," shouted the gunman.

"She's not strong enough to handle the sails in

this wind," Will yelled angrily, pushing past the gun levelled at him.

The gunman fell silent, unsure where to point his weapon, and Lisa watched as he prepared for the short turn, ducking, ready to move to the opposite seat. She looked at Will. He nodded. She turned the wheel and held her breath. The boom swept past her, and the gunman rose unsteadily to his feet to move to the opposite side of the boat. He was unprepared for Will tackling him and sending him back where he was. Their momentum caused the boat to lean even further, and the deck rails went into the water. A wave rolled over the edge and into the cockpit, soaking both men. Will was the bigger of the two, but his foe was wiry, and they rolled around awkwardly in the cockpit as Lisa held *Sea Mist* as steady as she could, keeping the sails full.

Lisa hardly heard the shot over the wind, but she saw Will fall back against the seat, cradling his right arm. Blood oozed through his slicker, joining the water running in rivulets down the yellow sleeve. "Will!"

"Keep this thing goin'," the gunman screeched, pointing the weapon at her as he rose from the floor. She watched him scramble up onto the upper deck and look out over the water, checking, she guessed, for the buoy which marked the international border. They were nowhere close to it yet, and she looked down at Will, slumped on the floor of the cockpit.

And a rage unlike any she had ever felt suddenly seethed inside her and bubbled to the surface; she could taste it in the back of her throat. She looked into Will's eyes and he nodded knowingly back at her, grabbing the rail of the nearby staircase with his good arm. Lisa looked back at the man standing on the deck, the man who had intruded so vilely upon their lives, and turned *Sea Mist* away from the howling wind.

She watched the boom pass over Will's head, as if in slow motion. It cut a perfect arc as it swept past her and hit the gunman squarely on his back with an unholy thud, snapping it in two as easily as breaking a toothpick. The breath knocked out of him, he couldn't even scream as he tumbled over the side and was swallowed whole by the Pacific.

...

Lisa threw the anchor into the shallow water of Sunset Bay, back at Carleton Island, and Will guided *Sea Mist* backward until it grabbed hold, then cut the engine. The boat began to drift as they folded the sails for the night, silent. They'd hardly spoken since the gunman had disappeared. They were intent only on getting to safe harbour. The western sky had darkened with a coming storm, and they could hear thunder in the distance. Sunset Bay was the closest, and so they had returned, despite what had started there that morning. They could not, however, bring themselves to dock again. They cleaned the blood out of the cockpit and descended into the cabin.

Will stood at the table, sighed heavily, and pulled off his sweater and long-sleeved T-shirt. The wound in his arm had looked a lot worse than it was. The bullet had only grazed him, though it stung like crazy from the salt water. The wound had stopped bleeding, but Lisa pulled out the medical kit and cleaned it up, applied a bandage. Then she surveyed the mess on the floor. There were dishes everywhere, in a soup of dirty dishwater. She got down on her knees and began picking them up, then spied the black duffel bag, long forgotten, against the wall under the table. She reached for it, hauled it out, and sat it on the table. Will was pulling his sweater back on. He looked at her questioningly, then into the bag. His gaze moved slowly back to her, still on her knees on the floor. Their eyes held for what seemed like an eternity.

Then Will smiled at her, and she smiled back. He leaned forward and kissed her on the forehead. He rose from the bench and stepped over to the cabinet where the navigational equipment was kept. He paused for a second to run his hands over the wood. Then he pulled out the radio log.

Lisa retrieved the mop and got working on the cleanup. She heard the radio come on and then Will talking to the coast guard, telling them what had happened. When he was finished, he recorded the call in the log and came up behind her.

"They're going to meet us back at Darnell Bay tomorrow," he said. "They'll need some more details from us, but we're not in trouble. And they'll take care of the money." His strong arms encircled her from behind. He held her close and she leaned her head against his shoulder. He kissed her on the neck. "I've been thinking," he said after several seconds had passed. "Why don't we give Gary a call as soon as we get home?"

She whirled around. "Do you mean it?"

He nodded and grinned. "After what we've been through today, I think we're capable of handling anything, even starting the business all over again."

Lisa looked once more into his green eyes. The life was back. She threw herself into his arms just as the first drops of rain splatted onto the deck.

Wishes

Melanie Hamilton was tired, staring-into-space tired. Her neck and shoulders ached from sitting at a desk all day and into the night, for the last five in a row. Her eyes were gritty; even the lids hurt. But the project was done in a week, a record for this particular client, and she could see the lights of Winton below, finally, reflected in dead-calm waters offshore. Her plane would touch down in minutes, her husband Rob would be there, and she would be home and in bed before midnight.

She held her breath as the runway rose to meet the small commuter, and she braced for the inevitable rough landing. She let out her breath slowly as the plane bumped along to the terminal building. She really hated this leg of the trip, even though it was the one to bring her home. Somehow the miracle of flight was less reassuring when you could feel every nuance of the air under the wings and tarmac under the tires. She reached for her purse at her feet and grabbed her lipstick from it. If she looked as bad as she felt, it was the least she could do for her husband.

But when Melanie walked into the tiny

arrivals area of the terminal building, Rob wasn't there. That was not unheard of. If he could make it, he would always be there to greet her. If not, he would leave her a message. She pulled her cell phone out of her purse and turned it on, but there was nothing in the display to alert her to a message. She flipped it open anyway, to see if she'd missed a call, but the digital display showed only the current day and time: Friday the 28th, 10:35 p.m.

It was possible Rob left the house late and was on his way, but it was odd that he didn't leave a message to say so. He was usually diligent about that sort of thing, though he could have forgotten to charge the battery on his phone and left the house in a hurry, not realizing it was dead. She watched for him while she waited for her luggage, then headed for the exit, pulling her suitcase behind her. If he was running late he might avoid the parking lot and wait for her out front.

But he was not out front, either. A number of vehicles were parked in the lot on the other side of the road, but she couldn't see them clearly with the outdoor lighting blazing above her head. Maybe he had been early and closed his eyes in the truck for a few minutes and fell asleep. He'd had a busy week, too, with three sets of buyers arriving to take possession of their new homes. She headed across the road. The truck should be easy to find, even outside the weak circles of light cast from poles at either end of the lot. The dogs would be watching for her from the crew cab and would bark as they always did, excited to see her.

She walked the entire first row of vehicles and then the second, past people she recognized from her flight getting their luggage into cars and driving away. In a very short time there were only airport staff vehicles sitting in reserved spots. She stopped and again pulled her phone from her purse, punched buttons, and put the phone to her ear. She grabbed the handle of her suitcase and started back to the terminal building, plastic wheels scritching on the concrete in the dead-quiet lot.

As she neared the doors, a female voice on her phone, one she didn't know, asked her to leave a message. She must have dialed the wrong number. She tried the house instead but her own voice asked for the same. She complied this time: "Hi, it's me. I'm at the airport. You forgot or got tied up. No problem. I'm going to get a taxi. I should be home shortly after midnight."

Inside, a pimply-faced young man in a ball cap was mopping the lino floor, and a wide woman with a long grey ponytail was wiping down the check-in counters. Melanie's flight was the last of the day. They glanced at her, surprised she was back but not interested enough to ask why. Just doing their jobs. There was no one else in the room. She used her phone to connect to the Internet, then searched for taxi companies in Winton. Three were listed but only the third one she called was willing to come for her at this late hour. Small towns. Gotta love 'em.

While she waited she tried Rob's cell again, but a woman's answering machine was still taking the call. "I must be more tired than I think," she muttered. There was still no answer at the house, either. If he was as exhausted as she was, she'd probably find him on the couch. She should have thought of getting a taxi in the first place.

The house was dark when the taxi pulled into the driveway, but when she headed to the front door she could hear Ben and Jerry barking, ever alert. She was soon inside, and the yellow Labs were there to greet her, dancing with excitement. She gave them each hugs and tummy rubs, happy to see them, too.

She turned on the front-hall light, glancing at the couch in the living room, knowing the dogs' ruckus would have woken Rob if he was there. The couch was empty. She checked the bedroom and the TV room. Nothing. It was not unusual for things to come up in his business that kept him down-island or up-island overnight: an emergency at one of the job sites or a new lot up for bid that he just had to have. She checked the hall table for a note, but there was nothing. He probably lost track of his days this week, didn't realize she was home tonight. She would check with his assistant in the morning.

If she didn't get her head on a pillow within the next few minutes, she would collapse where she stood.

...

Melanie woke at 10 a.m., her head fuzzy, eyes bleary. It would take more than one night's sleep to make up for the hellish week she'd had. She started coffee and then stood in a hot shower, washing away much of her exhaustion, emerging relatively refreshed. She drank her coffee in the sunshine on the deck and watched the dogs investigate the yard, checking if anything had happened overnight. She emptied her mind, finally, of the week's work and breathed in the fragrances of bare earth, green grass, and fir needles in her back yard. Her thoughts turned to Rob, but if he had remembered she was home, he'd know she'd have a late morning. He would probably call at lunch time.

Thirty minutes later she went inside and threw herself into the task of unpacking, rolling her suitcase from the front door to the bedroom and heaving it up onto the bed. She grabbed her laundry bag and carried it to the wicker hamper she kept in the ensuite bathroom. To her surprise the hamper was empty. "That's odd," she said aloud to the four-legged bookends watching her from the doorway. "Daddy doesn't do laundry." And she'd been gone a week. She emptied the bag into the hamper and went to the dresser, wanting to witness the miracle that was Rob's clean and folded laundry within it. But when she opened his T-shirt drawer she saw her own T-shirts instead.

Melanie stared at the coloured piles, and a little something fluttered in her stomach. She opened another drawer, and another, and all she saw were her own clothes, neatly folded and arranged. The little something started doing backflips. She hurried to the bedroom closet.

Suits, blouses, pants, skirts—all hers—filled the space, hanging neatly and unencumbered. She raced to the front door, curious dogs on her heels. Nothing of Rob's in the closet there, either. She headed downstairs to his home office and stopped dead at the doorway. Instead of Rob's huge oak desk and table, worn leather chair, and dented filing cabinets, there was a set of twin beds with a chest of drawers between them. She sat on the end of one of them, a high-pitched squealing in her ears and dark pinpoints popping in her eyes.

"What the hell is going on?" she asked Ben and Jerry when she raised her head from between her knees. "Where's Daddy?" Two big heads tilted in response to the question. They had no answer for her.

The unimaginable was playing with her mind, and she tried to dismiss it. But the fact remained: there was no trace of her husband anywhere. She went to one last door in the house, the one to the garage. Her black Pathfinder, shiny and clean, sat inside, alone. She turned to the wall at her left; the workbench was clean except for ceramic pots she wanted to find plants for. All the garden tools hung in a row next to the bench, and all the household tools were in their place, soldiers at attention, on the wall above and down the bench's length. Rob never kept it this neat and tidy. Could he have hired someone to come in and fix everything up, thinking it would soften the blow?

If he had left her, that is.

There was no other explanation.

Melanie went to the phone on the hall table to call Rob's secretary. "Hi, Paula. It's me. Can you tell me where Rob is?"

"I'm sorry, but you must have the wrong number. There's no Paula here."

"I must have dialled incorrectly. Sorry to bother you."

Melanie checked the number and dialled again.

"Paula?"

"No, I'm sorry. You've reached the same number again. This is the McVay residence— Patrick and Tina McVay."

She hung up and stared at the phone in its cradle. He changed his office number? She tried Rob's cell number. The voice from the night before answered, but this time it was the real thing. Her body stiffened.

It wasn't possible.

He had promised.

She gritted her teeth. "Is Rob there?"

"Sorry, there's no Rob here."

"But you have his phone," she said between tight lips. "I called his number."

"Excuse me? This is *my* phone. I've had this number for six years!"

"Who is this?" Melanie's voice was shaking. "What's your name?"

"I don't have to tell you that. You have the wrong number!" And the woman hung up.

What was happening?

The doorbell rang, causing her to jump and the dogs to race to the front door. It was her neighbour and best friend, Gail, who stepped in to keep the dogs from escaping, then hugged them up like old pals.

"How were the guys when you got home last night?" Gail asked.

"Good. Excited to see me, as usual."

"I tried to keep them busy all week so they wouldn't miss you too much."

"You've kept them busy all week? Where was Rob?"

"Rob?"

"Did he ask you to take care of them for him?"

A frown creased Gail's brow. "Did you ask someone else to take care of Ben and Jerry this time?"

"No, of course not. But I thought Rob would have them all week."

"I don't know who Rob is, Mel," Gail said, and then a grin slowly spread across her face. "Are you keeping secrets from me? Have you met someone? I want to hear everything!"

Melanie stared at her friend, her tired brain a muddle, struggling to speak. "Uhhh, what are you talking—?"

"Sorry, Mel," Gail said suddenly, looking at her watch. "Got an appointment and I'm already late. We'll talk later!" She gave both dogs a pat on the head and quickly went out the door, closing it behind her.

Melanie fumbled with the bolt. She stood in the foyer, staring at the slate floor. Something was going on.

And then the corners of her mouth turned up and her hands went to her cheeks. "Oh my goodness!" she said aloud, and Ben and Jerry bounced around her, joining in on her apparent excitement.

It was her birthday.

And true to form, her husband and her best friend were pulling a fast one on her. This was by far the most elaborate hoax she'd ever seen them create, but it was her fortieth, after all. She and Rob had planned to celebrate after she got home. Gail would be on the phone right now, telling him about the look on her face. "They think they're being funny," she said to the dogs, "and they are, a little." But Rob wouldn't guess what she had been thinking, and Gail didn't know about his past transgression.

She couldn't believe she fell for it. The super cleanup was part of the joke. She'd once shared with Gail a fantasy she had: one where Rob's mess was out of the house, she had all the drawers and closet space to herself, and everything always stayed neat and tidy, the way she liked it. She dreamed of having a whole day to herself, the house, even the bed, to herself. Today, everything in the house was where it should be, everything was clean and tidy, and the whole place had been hers since she arrived home last night, just after midnight. They must have been planning this for weeks. It was a great birthday surprise!

The next thing would be the party. She was

dying to call Gail, but she didn't want to spoil it for her. She settled in her home office instead, catching up after a week away, and watched the clock. They would be expecting her to take the dogs to the park at the usual time this afternoon and hit the fitness club after that. She'd get home just in time for the big barbeque!

...

Melanie stood in front of the mirror at the club, drying her hair, flushed from her workout and hot shower, and excited. Undoubtedly Rob and Gail had a house full of people waiting for her and a mile-high pile of ribs ready to put on the barbeque. Of course, she wouldn't spoil the surprise, as much as she'd get great satisfaction in telling them she was onto them. With all the work they'd done in the house? It was worth letting them have their fun.

The street was quiet when she pulled into the garage, as she expected. Everyone would be parked well away to throw her off. After she pulled into the garage and got out of the SUV, she pressed the button to roll the big door back down. She unlocked the door to the back hall and cocked her ear as she pushed it open, but there wasn't a sound. Only Ben and Jerry sitting on the carpet, their tails slapping in rhythm. She then slipped into the laundry room with her gym bag and took a minute at the mirror over the washtub to wipe the grin off her face, donning the innocent and serious face that would fool her guests into thinking they'd fooled her.

But when she turned the corner into the living room, only the eager faces of the two dogs greeted her, looking for their supper early, as always. She peeked into the kitchen and then went to the bedroom, calling to her husband. Nothing. She headed downstairs. No one. Glanced out into the yard.

She was absolutely alone.

...

Melanie sat in bed, two pillows behind her back and a book lying unopened in her lap. Ben and Jerry took up the majority of the space, eyes closed in utter contentment and innocence, paws twitching with dreams. She stared at the dogs. They were her only reality since arriving home the night before. Her eyes wouldn't close, her brain wouldn't give up. She'd been over and over it. He couldn't be gone. Why would he go? They were happy. Everything was as it should be.

She had wracked her brain for hours trying to

remember if Rob had said or done anything that could have led her to believe he would do this. She'd drawn a blank. There had been no hint of anything wrong. She was mystified. In fact she didn't quite believe yet that her husband had left her. The way he had done it made no sense. The birthday surprise suddenly seemed a cruel joke.

Then a glimmer of hope appeared. What if this was all part of the plan? After all, a full day alone wasn't officially over for a little while yet. Maybe Rob would arrive home at the stroke of midnight. He'd tell her the barbeque was tomorrow instead, and they'd have a good laugh over how he'd fooled her.

"Yeah, right," she said aloud. She was kidding herself.

She had been tempted to call Gail several times since getting home from the fitness club, but something kept her from doing so. Not that she thought Gail had anything to do with Rob's leaving. She had never seen anything between them; she wasn't Rob's type.

Rob's type. Melanie snuggled under the covers, turned onto her side, and stroked a big dog body lying next to her. She hadn't thought about the affair for a while. The pain was duller now; everything was good between them. He had fulfilled his promise to make it up to her. But it still lingered there, in the background, what he was capable of, just in case she became too secure. He had told her he drank too much one night, when she was away on another contract, while celebrating completion of a house project with a woman he'd worked with on the design. He said it was all about the booze and it would never happen again.

The night he told her about it, she lay awake, wanting him out of her life. To her, an affair was the ultimate betrayal. She was going to turn forty the next year. She would still be young enough to meet someone else. She made a wish for her fortieth birthday: to be rid of him.

Melanie suddenly sat upright in bed, startling the dogs. They jumped off and ran out of the room, low growls in their throats, looking for the disturbance. "No, no, no," she said, shaking her head, not believing what she was thinking. "It's not possible."

Suddenly she froze. Something swished against the door. A prickling started on the back of her neck and rose in a wave to the top of her head. She stared, wide-eyed, in the door's direction, expecting some ethereal being to appear, waft toward her, and admonish her for things not carefully wished for.

But it was only Ben and Jerry. Of course. They jumped back onto the bed, and a nervous giggle escaped her mouth. And then the tears came. Rob was gone. She lay back on the pillow and, as the clock in the living room began to chime the midnight hour, she made a wish.

...

Melanie woke early. She had an appointment at 10 a.m. with a new client and needed to review the company information, rehearse her presentation. One look in the mirror told her she'd need a big mug of coffee this morning. She felt like she'd been through the wringer all night. An intense dream she couldn't remember.

By the time she'd showered and dressed and prepared for her meeting, she was rushing. She ushered Ben and Jerry out to the back yard, gave them a pat each, and assured them she wouldn't be gone long this time. A local client was a nice change. She knew that her tone of voice was enough to convince them, and they trotted off to reaffirm the property perimeter.

She carried the directions to the client's office

in her lap as she drove; it was a little off the beaten path, in a new area of town. But she was there on time, and the big sign at the entrance confirmed she was in the right place.

The mobile office was a first for her. She climbed the raw wooden stairs in front and stepped through the open door. It was stifling inside, a large fan at one end doing its best to move the hot air. At the other end of the small room sat a large oak desk and a number of dented filing cabinets, both strewn with papers. A man rose from a worn leather chair and came around to greet her.

She extended her hand to him. "Hello, I'm Melanie Brewster." His hand felt warm and comfortable in hers, familiar somehow.

"Hello, Melanie," he replied. "Nice to meet you. I'm Rob Hamilton."

Syl and Sam

Syl struggled to keep awake at the wheel as she drove along the straight, flat, and seemingly endless prairie highway. She wasn't used to it after living in the mountains for twenty-five years. The few hours' drive from the airport in a rental car was more than enough for her. The large cup of coffee she had picked up on her way out of the city helped for a while, but it was now gone. She turned up the volume on the radio and forced herself to glance away from the unchanging asphalt ahead to the almost unchanging landscape on either side. Occasionally there was a farmyard corralled by trees to hold back the shifting soil. Sometimes a pasture enclosed by barbed-wire fencing. Mostly golden lakes of rippling wheat.

A grasshopper hit the car's windshield, causing her to jump in her seat. It bounced off the glass directly in front of her and left a green hind leg behind. Some nondescript goo held it in place at one end, the other buffeted by the wind. Syl hoped the rest of it cleared the car. She flipped on the windshield washer and the leg disappeared. At least in an ideal world. She shuddered at the thought of coming across its remnants on the outside of the door. She'd have to ask someone to clean it off for her. Seriously. It was a phobia. She sent a silent prayer to the heavens. If the farm was covered with the dead grasshopper's brethren, she wouldn't be able to get out of the car. She'd have to turn around and go back to the airport.

But that wouldn't go over well with *anyone*.

It appeared the grasshopper was alone, just in the wrong place at the wrong time. No infestation, no worst nightmare, and no excuse not to be at the family reunion. As Syl turned onto a secondary road her heart began to accelerate anyway, and her grip tightened on the wheel. She was less than a half hour away, only two more turns ahead, and her stress level was getting away from her. Though she was close to her four brothers—they had a family history together, at least—she had little in common with their wives. While her parents were alive, her sisters-in-law were polite to her, and she to them, but after her parents died—first her dad, then her mom—a couple of them came into their own. And things weren't so polite anymore.

Syl glanced in the rear-view mirror as she

came to the turnoff to the narrower road on which the family farm, now her oldest brother Phil's, stood. No other car was coming up behind her, there was no one ahead, and no one approached her on Phil's road. That was the prairies for you. Desolate. She made the turn, but then pulled over to the side of the road as far as she could and stopped. A little farther and she could tip the car onto its hood in the deep ditch. Disappear for a while. It was attractive, but the potential for getting hurt prevented her from doing so. Getting hurt wouldn't help her get through the weekend, only detract from its purpose. She guessed that wouldn't help her already deteriorating relationships within the family.

She sat for a short five minutes with the air-conditioning blowing in her face, gathering happy thoughts, mustering determination, pasting her loving-sister-and-caring-aunt face on. Trying not to think about what the hours ahead could hold. She lowered the sun visor to reveal a mirror, applied fresh lipstick, and ran her hands through her cropped hair. And then she straightened herself in her seat, thrust her shoulders back, and pulled back onto the road. She was minutes away.

Syl spotted it in the distance, the third farmyard from the turnoff, on the left. The house was hidden by trees on this approach, but she'd know it by the feel of the road. After all, she and her brothers grew up here. And there was the wind turbine Phil told her about, installed since she last visited. She slowed the car to make the turn into the farmyard and took a deep breath. Her internal stopwatch started ticking.

There were already a number of vehicles nosed in to the four-foot cotoneaster hedge that bordered the lawn at the front of the house, a two-storey home ordered from the Eaton's catalogue by her grandparents in the early twentieth century, then passed to her parents. Phil's wife Claire had seen to numerous renovations, of course. The house still had the same basic layout, but it was definitely not her parents' home anymore. Porches had become rooms, two bathrooms had been added, and then there was the huge wooden deck attached to three sides. The siding on the house was still white, but the shutters on the windows were now tangerine.

Syl pulled in beside a black pickup that would require a ladder for her to climb into. No doubt it belonged to one of her nephews. She climbed out of the car and strode purposefully to the concrete slab walkway leading to the front door. She was empty-handed for now, not sure where she would be put for the weekend: in one of the three spare bedrooms upstairs in the house, or doubled up with one of her brothers' families in a camper out back.

Two little girls in matching pink shorts and striped T-shirts glanced at her as they ran by, ponytails swinging back and forth in little-girl rhythm. Syl called to them, "Hi, there!" but they didn't respond or stop, just disappeared around the side of the house. She was pretty sure they were her brother Russ's granddaughters. Over the years she had dutifully looked at the pictures all her sisters-in-law sent her so she wouldn't make any mistakes. She had met everyone on previous visits, but she had lived away from the prairies for a long time. She hardly knew her nieces and nephews, let alone their children. And they certainly didn't know their aunt Syl.

No one came out the front door of the house to greet her; she assumed they were all in back. She caught a glimpse of a big white tent through the trees as she walked in that direction. It was the only way everyone could be together in the same place at the same time, for meals mostly. She followed the path of her two grand-nieces, past Claire's planters overflowing with hardy petunias—bursts of purple and pink and white—and entered the yard behind the house. She made a wide berth around a small grasshopper clinging to the white siding near the corner and hoped no one saw her do it. The family teenagers were sitting around the open barbeque pit on the other side of the tent, consumed with each other and all sorts of barking family dogs, who were begging them to chuck the ball they were teasing them with.

Claire's backyard gardens had expanded considerably since Syl was last here. Masses of colour and scent. It was no small feat to have such a beautiful garden when the primary water source on the farm was a prairie slough and the drying summer wind never stopped blowing. She noticed the black tubes of a watering system snaking their way throughout the beds, and she heard the gurgling of running water and spotted several small decorative fountains placed among the flowers.

Someone behind Syl called her name, and she

turned toward the voice. It was Sherry, wife of her youngest brother, Tim, exiting the back door of the house. Sherry approached her, a smile on her face, and gave her a big hug. "You look great!" she said. "Love the hair!"

Syl hugged her back. Last time Sherry saw her, her hair was fake brown, but she was now all natural, mostly white above and grey at the nape. "I got tired of keeping Miss Clairol in business!" she said.

Sherry chuckled. "Well, I think it's great, and the short-and-sassy do is perfect on you."

"Thanks, Sherry. And you look fabulous!"

"Thank you! I've started early on my diet, determined to look great for the boys' wedding next year."

"You never have to worry about that," said Syl. "You always look great." She meant it. Sherry was one of those natural beauties, fair-haired and freckled, unspoiled by makeup, brown from hours in the summer sun tending her yard in the city, her thick blond hair bleached almost white. Happiness written all over her face. No one would ever notice her weight. "Where are the boys?"

"In the tent, I think. Come and meet the fiancés. You'll love them. They're very creative, just like you. You should hear what they've already come up with for the wedding." Sherry looped her arm through Syl's, and they walked to the tent. Easy going like her husband, Sherry was by far Syl's favourite sister-in-law. She was a teacher, like Tim, and their twin boys were teachers too. If that wasn't enough, the boys were marrying twin sisters—interior designers in business together—and at the same place and time. A double wedding. A tiny dread tickled Syl's insides as she thought of attending yet another family event next year.

The din of adult voices and excited children greeted them when they entered the tent. Russ's wife, Janet, looked up at them from her seat at one of the long tables. She had the pony-tailed girls in pink on either side of her and colouring books and piles of crayons spread in front. Syl smiled and said, "Hi, Janet," to her but she was already turned back to the table, preoccupied with her granddaughters. Syl didn't take it personally. Janet was the least social of her brothers' wives, kept mostly to herself and her own family, and always looked completely overwhelmed.

"Look who's here," said Sherry as she led Syl

over to her sons, who stood with two indistinguishable but beautiful olive-skinned women. Both boys stepped forward and gave Syl a hug. The two introduced her to their brides-to-be, who apparently parted their long dark hair on different sides so people could tell them apart. The boys had made it easy for her: one liked facial hair while the other did not. It worked. They assured her that once she got to know their girls, she'd easily see their differences. Syl wondered to herself when they thought she'd have that chance, given they lived so far away from her.

Syl spotted her four brothers standing together next to a long table on the other side of the tent, each with a bottle of beer in hand. She excused herself from the circle of twins and walked in their direction. But they didn't see her coming, and before she could reach them Claire appeared abruptly in front of her.

"Sylvia," she said. "You're here. I wasn't sure you'd show up." She glanced at Syl's hair, said nothing.

Syl looked at Claire's perfectly made-up face and freshly coloured coiffure. "Of course I'm here. I'm not going to miss the reunion. So, where would you like me to sleep?"

"That's a good question. Let me think." Claire paused, furrowed her brow, and pursed her lips, patting the latter with manicured and pink-polished fingernails, trying to look like she was unprepared for this turn of events. Despite Syl having e-mailed her plans to her. Syl was not fooled. Claire was always prepared.

"While you're thinking I'll go say hello to my brothers."

Claire stopped her before she had taken a step. "You can have one of the bedrooms in the house, I guess. The back one. I'll have to put the two boys in together. That would be the easiest." Her two youngest grandsons. The same arrangement as last time.

"Okay!" Syl tried to carry on to her brothers, but Claire continued to block her way.

"Let's do this now, Sylvia, while I have a minute."

Syl looked over to the four men. Phil had spotted her now. He shrugged his shoulders meekly, his free hand stuck in his jeans pocket, and went back to his conversation. "You go ahead and do what you have to do, Claire. I can move myself into the room later." She edged past her sister-in-law and continued on the path she started. The corner of her mouth twitched when she heard Claire hit a body part against a metal folding chair as she attempted to storm out of the tent. Storming didn't work well on grass.

"I see you've annoyed my wife," Phil said in her ear as he hugged her. "Why do you do that? Isn't it just easier to do what she wants?"

"It may be easier, big brother, but not as much fun." Phil smirked at her. It had been clear to Syl from day one that he had chosen the easier path with Claire, but she didn't hold it against him. He had to live with her.

And then her other three brothers hugged her—first Tim, who then stood back and let Don and Russ move in together to sandwich her, as always. She was number three in the birth order. They were numbers two and four. A mining engineer and a large-animal veterinarian, respectively, but they'd been doing this to her since they were kids. She braced for impact and the chorus of splatting, burping, and farting noises they liked to make to effect squishing her to bursting. And then they released her and laughed like it was the first time they'd ever done it. She laughed along, because it gave the three of them something special together.

But Syl had never felt like she fit her brothers' sandwich well. As an artist, a painter, she couldn't be further away from any of her brothers in temperament, something that always seemed lost on them. She hadn't been part of their world growing up: playing cowboys and Indians, hunting gophers with BB guns, and doing outside chores. Instead, she had been inside with her mother, learning to cook and sew and keep a home, yes, but also exploring her creativity.

For her mother had been an artist, too. Her passion was photography, but real life and a large family on a farm got in the way of her pursuing it professionally, though at one time the walls of the house were covered with her work. She and her daughter tried every art and craft they could together, intent on determining what Syl was passionate about, and if there was any time at all left in the day, they explored the farm and took pictures. Syl owed her artistic eye to those special hours they spent together in the fields and the many groves of trees, often on their backs or their knees.

Tim now brought Syl a glass of cold, dark beer, the head slightly overflowing and sliding down the outside, and the siblings stood together, easily falling into conversation about old times, despite their differences. As they always had, as if it was just the five of them again. They may not have understood their sister, but they were taught by their mother to respect her.

Tim finally addressed the elephant in the tent: "How's everything going on the Island?" She knew what he was fishing for. She had informed all her brothers a few months ago that she was divorcing her husband, finally, after thirty years, but talking on the phone about it was far easier than facing them in person.

"Everything's going fine," she replied.

"You should have left him years ago," Russ piped in. Of course she should have.

"If he gives you any trouble, just let me know," Don added.

"He won't, don't worry," she replied quickly. She wouldn't put it past any, or all, of her brothers to pay her ex a visit. They had always been fiercely protective of her as a child. It frustrated them that she lived so far away, but she knew it had been the best thing for her all those years ago, to be surrounded by a burgeoning community of artists. And they didn't know the whole truth. They thought she finally got a backbone and threw him out, but it was her husband who wanted to go. She hadn't cared about the new fling, there'd been many over the years, more than her brothers knew about, but this one he wanted to marry. It was easier on her to let them believe what they wanted to believe.

Syl scrambled to change the subject, just as Phil's youngest son, accompanied by a half dozen of the young children, suddenly appeared at Phil's elbow. "Hey, Dad, the kids are bugging me for a ride on the tractor. Has the old Deere got some fuel in it?"

"Yeah, and it's got the bucket on it and the flat behind. They should get a kick out of that. But only in the yard, slow and easy."

"You got it." The kids screeched in excitement and raced out of the tent.

And then Claire was back, soliciting Phil and Don's help to move the barbecue where she wanted it, successfully breaking up the sibling circle, ignoring Syl altogether. Syl decided to head to her car for her bag and get settled in the back bedroom for the weekend.

...

When Syl descended the staircase from the bedroom fifteen minutes later she found a grand-niece in the living room, sitting cross legged on the carpeted floor between couch and coffee table. Her long brown hair obscured her face and, intent on what she was doing, she was unaware of her great-aunt's arrival. As Syl approached she saw that the child was drawing with pencil on a letter-size piece of lined white paper, her head bobbing up and down as she reproduced her subject. Syl glanced over to see what it was: a stuffed brown teddy bear sitting on the floor in front of the TV, facing the artist.

"Hello," said Syl to the girl, who startled and quickly turned her paper over before looking up. Her dark eyes were wide, and strands of hair were caught on her nose; she pushed them back. Syl knew this one: Don's granddaughter. She was unsure of her age—under ten, she thought. She didn't have the kids' ages in her head, but she shuffled the photos Don's wife, Angela, emailed to her recently to find her name. "Are you Samantha?" she asked.

"Sam," the girl murmured.

"Do you remember me?" The child paused. "I'm your great-aunt Syl. Your grandpa's sister."

"Your hair is different."

"Yours is, too. It's longer than I remember."

"Mom wants me to cut it, but I like it long."

"I do, too. I had hair like yours when I was your age. My mom wanted *me* to cut it, too. She said it would be easier, but I think long is easier because you can put it in a ponytail or in braids."

"Me too!"

Syl had the girl's attention. She sat on the couch next to her. "May I see your drawing?"

Sam spread her hands protectively over her paper. "It's not very good."

"I didn't think *my* first drawings were very good either, but they got better and better the more I did."

"I thought you were a painter."

"I am, but most of my paintings start with drawings."

"I don't have any paints," said Sam, looking down at her hands.

"Would you like to try some of mine while I'm here this weekend? I brought some with me. We could try painting the teddy bear you're drawing."

Sam looked up at her and smiled wide, and two dimples popped up in her cheeks. "Sure!" And then she turned her paper over and handed her drawing to Syl.

Syl was struck by the likeness of the drawn

bear to the real thing, given her niece's age, and was about to tell her so, knowing how much she yearned for affirmation herself at that age. But an impatient voice pre-empted her: "Sam! Why are you inside?" Syl and Sam simultaneously turned their heads toward the speaker. It was Angela, Sam's grandmother, her face stern, all her sharp angles showing. "Your uncle's doing tractor rides with the other kids. Go have some fun!"

"I *am* having fun, Grandma," said Sam.

Angela came over and stood in front of her granddaughter, blocking her view of the teddy bear. "I mean *outside*, Sam. You should be outside on such a beautiful day, with the other kids."

"But I don't want a tractor ride."

Syl rose to her feet. "How about a walk, then, Sam? We artists need to get some ideas for our next drawings."

Sam got to her feet. "Sure!"

"Don't get it into her head about being an artist, Sylvia," said Angela. "That's not what her parents want for her."

Syl looked down at Sam's face, its waning smile. "It's too late, Angela. She's *already* an artist." And she put her hand out to Sam, who gripped it with a ferocity that made Syl's spine tingle. "Let's go upstairs and get my camera, Sam. And then we'll be off!"

"Sylvia, you should mind your own business."

"Oddly enough, Angela, this *is* my business," said Syl. And with that she and Sam headed to the stairs.

Minutes later they were on their way out the front door, avoiding the rest of the family in the back. "Where are we going, Aunty Sylvia?" asked Sam as they walked across the driveway.

Syl reached her hand out and Sam grabbed it. "I have a secret place on the farm all my own, and I'm going to share it with you. Only you. You can't tell anyone about it, not even your mom and dad or your grandma and grandpa. Can you promise you'll keep it a secret?"

"Yes!" Sam's eagerness showed in her bright eyes, and her happiness in being singled out as special was reflected in her toothy smile. She looked quickly to the far side of the yard, where the excited cries of the other children on the tractor ride could barely be heard over the engine. Syl knew she wanted to be sure the other children didn't see them, but they weren't even looking their way. "Where is it?" Sam asked conspiratorially.

"You'll see. But we're going to use our artist eyes to look for interesting things along the way."

"What interesting things?"

"We won't know until we see them."

"And we're going to take pictures of them?"

"That's right."

"And then we're going to draw them?"

"That's right."

"And then we're going to paint them?"

Syl laughed. "That's right, Sam, if we think they should be painted. Sometimes drawings are okay just the way they are."

Syl led Sam to the ditch beyond the dirt yard, which was bordered by the hedgerow of thick caraganas that surrounded the home quarter. The dirt path was mostly hidden by dry wild grasses at this time of year, but Syl didn't need to see it. She created it herself with the many trips she made to her secret place as a child and every time she visited home as an adult. She could find it with her eyes closed.

When they reached the ditch, Syl let go of Sam's hand, knowing the path to be too narrow to walk beside each other. "Follow me," she said as she stepped onto it and into the shade of the hedgerow, "but let me know if you see something interesting!" The light breeze brought the smells of childhood summers—rich dark earth and ripened wheat—to her nostrils, and she breathed deeply, her shoulders relaxing. She walked briskly, revelling in her new responsibility to guide the artist inside the little girl walking behind her.

"Aunty Sylvia, look!"

Syl stopped and turned. Sam squatted on the trail, staring at something through the grass. "Have you found something interesting, Sam?"

"Yup, a grasshopper!"

A grasshopper. Syl's heart leapt to her throat. Suddenly she couldn't make her feet move to join her grand-niece.

Sam looked up. "What's wrong, Aunty? Don't you want to see it? It's *very* interesting. Look." And her hand disappeared into the grass as she pointed to it. She looked back at Syl. "Don't be afraid. It won't jump. It's eating the grass."

Syl smiled nervously. "How do you know I'm afraid of it?"

"Because you look like I do when I see a garter snake."

"A garter snake? At least snakes can't jump and land in your hair!"

"But they can slither up your pants!"

Syl chuckled. "I never thought of that." And suddenly she reached for her camera in the cloth bag slung over her shoulder and, before she could think about it, took the few steps to Sam and squatted beside her.

The grasshopper was two feet away, a relatively comfortable distance, Syl told herself. Even better, it was oblivious to her and Sam, so intent was it on devouring grass. As she zoomed in on it and it grew in her lens, she realized it *was* interesting. Beautiful even. Multi-textured, stripes and spots, variations of colour all over its body. To her, grasshoppers had always been either green or brown, but she guessed that's because she was too busy fleeing from them to notice otherwise. She took a number of shots in close succession. "It *is* interesting, Sam," she said. She handed the camera to Sam. "You look with the camera now, see it close up. Take as many pictures as you want." And she showed her the buttons to press on her digital camera.

"I like all the different colours," said Sam as she drew the LED screen toward her face.

"Me too. I've never seen one close up before." A memory dropped into her consciousness as soon as she'd spoken the words. She *had* seen one close up before. Russ dropped one in her hair when she was five. It had gotten tangled in the long, thick strands, and she had run screaming to her mother in the house. But that one was dead by the time her mother had disentangled it and shown it to her, and she hadn't looked at it very closely, her terror overwhelming her instead.

"I have, in a jar," said Sam, "but I mean the grass. It's all different colours of green and brown."

The grass. The child saw the grasshopper in context, pictured it in a frame. She already saw things like an artist, the details as well as the big picture. She was Syl herself at that age. Syl's mother had realized it about *her* too.

Syl's eyes pricked with tears, and she rose and took a few steps up the path while Sam was busy clicking pictures. The life of an artist was ahead of this grand-niece. The excitement, the obsession, the disappointment, the struggle. Surrounded mostly by people who didn't understand you. "But it's worth it," she whispered to herself, "to be who you are." And she would see to it that Sam knew that.

Sam was suddenly behind her. "I think we've

got enough pictures of the grasshopper, Aunty." She handed the camera back to her.

"Okay, then let's keep going!" Syl was eager to reach one of her favourite "interesting things" on the farm. After another thirty steps or so, she made a turn to the left out of the ditch and through a space in the hedgerow that marked the northeast corner of the home quarter. Here lay the subjects of many of her paintings over the years: the remains of old wooden granaries and derelict farm machinery dating to as long ago as her great-grandparents' time. Horse-drawn plow and swather, an old grain wagon mostly collapsed on the remains of its wooden wheels, and remnants of younger tractors and a combine. Other bits and pieces she didn't recognize at all.

A limitless number of possibilities for her as an artist, given the changes that occurred over the last forty years she'd been drawing and painting them. Even her mother had photographed them. Infinite shades of burnt-orange from rust eating at the metal, holes of all shapes and sizes, bolts and nails and chains for texture. The whole lot leaning in the wild grasses and flowers, as well as occasional wayward wheat and barley, and gradually being swallowed by the earth. The glorious sun casting dark shadows that changed it by the minute.

"Aunty Sylvia, is this your secret place?" Sam was as excited to see it as Syl was. She hurried from item to item, bending and looking.

"No, but it's a place with lots of ideas for us, so we'll stay here a little while before we go to my secret place."

"I didn't know this stuff was here. Mom and Dad don't allow me to leave the yard."

Syl glanced in the direction of the farmyard. The backs of the outbuildings were only about a hundred steps from where she stood, and they formed a sort of boundary around the yard, shielding this graveyard of machinery from view. But a farm was made for exploring. Even her brothers did that, though they were usually hunting gophers or rabbits, or looking for arrowheads. To not allow a child to explore on a farm was to deprive them of a chance to experience and learn things on their own. Children were far too sheltered these days.

Syl pulled out a water bottle and some cookies she had stashed in her bag, as well as the camera and a clipboard with a pad of plain white paper and a soft lead pencil attached to it. "Have a drink of water and a cookie, Sam, and tell me if you'd like to take pictures or draw something here. Sam chose the camera, as Syl thought she would, and hurriedly took a drink of water and wolfed down a cookie. "Just be careful walking around here," said Syl. "And don't get underneath anything or squeeze into anything. I don't want you to get hurt."

"I'll be careful," said Sam.

"I know you will."

Then Sam was off to explore. Syl took up the pad of paper and sat down on the remains of a wooden granary wall. But what she drew was wildly different from her usual: a little girl bent over the blade of an old plow, a camera in her hands, her brow furrowed with concentration, her ponytail falling over her shoulder. Syl rarely painted figures, but she knew now the first thing she was going to work on as soon as she got home.

An hour later, Syl was on her knees, wishing she'd worn long pants, crawling under the low-hanging branches of the willow grove that encircled her secret place. Not the first, not the second, but the third grove sitting between two wheat fields on Phil's property. A right turn from the hedgerow and a good two hundred steps from the machinery graveyard. Sam, also on her knees, passed her in her eagerness to see what was inside. Syl arrived to find her standing in the flat, open middle of the grove, looking up, the sun dappling her with leaf shadows.

"I can see why you picked this for your secret place," said Sam as she twirled in the sun. "No one would ever know it's here, so you can be by yourself." Exactly, thought Syl. She watched as Sam explored the space, and she shook her head in wonder. She had more in common with this child than anyone else in her entire family.

"What's in here?" asked Sam. She'd found the large plastic storage tub Syl hauled here when she was her age. Though the exterior colour, once blue, had dulled to grey, it had withstood more than forty years in the outdoors.

"All kinds of things," replied Syl. "Anything an artist might find interesting to draw."

"So you don't have to bring stuff with you every time you come."

"That's right."

"Can we open it?"

"Of course!" Syl joined Sam at the tub. "Let's drag it into the sun."

First, they removed the bungee cords that were holding the lid down to discourage inquisitive animals. And when Syl removed the lid, Sam gasped at all the goodies inside. She ooohed and aaahed at the old dolls, their clothes faded by the sun, and the stuffed animals. She tried out the pillow on the three-legged stool Syl's father had shortened for his daughter to sit on while she drew. There were discarded toys her brothers had broken and even a tea pot her mother hadn't wanted anymore. There were a number of small boxes filled with anything and everything tiny. And her mother had insisted on an old blanket, in case Syl got cold, and an umbrella, in case it rained.

Syl pulled out and sat on the folded blanket and watched Sam remove every item from the tub and study each, even if only briefly. She breathed deeply. It was nice and cool here in the protection of the trees. Even the birds knew it; she could hear them scurrying and scratching in the dirt.

"Did you come here every day when you were my age, Aunty?"

"No, I couldn't in the winter because it was too cold, and sometimes I had too many chores to do in the summer. I still tried to do at least a little bit of drawing or painting every day at home."

"My mom doesn't like me to do too much drawing."

"What does she like you to do?"

"Play with my friends."

"Oh." It was going to be tougher for Sam. Syl's mother had encouraged her art, had no problem with her being who she was—a loner.

"I wish I had a secret place," said Sam.

Syl did too, but how could Sam ever manage it without the support of her parents? Syl's parents knew about her secret place right from the beginning, as they had to know where to find her. But they also understood that she needed to be alone sometimes, away from her four brothers. Sam had brothers too, one older, one younger. It likely wasn't easy for her being the only girl, and a middle child, just like her great-aunt Syl.

Syl saw the dimples in Sam's face start to fade and she quickly jumped in. "Well, from now on, you *have* a secret place. You have *my* secret place. It's yours *and* mine now."

The dimples reappeared. "Really?"

"Really. Now, how about we each choose something to draw, and then we'd better get back to the house. It's getting close to suppertime."

...

It was nearly five o'clock when Syl and Sam walked into the white tent together, a little weary but happy. They'd eaten the rest of the cookies and drank the rest of the water while at the secret place, but Syl suspected Sam was as hungry as she was. The tables were covered in plastic cloths in primary colours, and matching paper plates, napkins, and cups were set up on the buffet table at the front of the tent, as were beverages of all kinds, for children and adults. Grainy bread, cheddar cheese, and sweet pickles were piled high on trays and covered in plastic wrap.

"Sam!" shouted someone inside. Sam's mother, Kirsten, came rushing toward them from a group of adults milling about the centre of the tent. She bent down to her daughter, her face in Sam's. "Where have you been, young lady? We've been waiting for you!"

"I was with Aunty Sylvia, Mom," Sam replied easily, but she took Syl's hand nevertheless.

Kirsten glanced up at Syl, but then went back to her daughter. "All afternoon? You've been gone for hours!"

"We were doing our . . . art," Sam said hesitantly.

"What have I told you about that, Sam?"

Sam didn't answer. Syl started to say something, but Kirsten interrupted her: "I don't want to hear from you right now, Aunt Sylvia." Her attention remained on Sam. "You need to tell me where you're going, Sam. I need to know where you are at all times."

"Grandma knew," said Sam in a barely audible voice.

"What?"

"Angela knew she was with me," said Syl. She looked over to the adults, now awkwardly quiet and watching them.

Angela was standing next to Don, who turned his head to look at her. She ignored him and made eye contact with Syl. "I knew she was with Sylvia, but I didn't know where they were," she said defensively.

"Where were you, Sam?" Kirsten asked again.

Sam looked up at Syl, still holding her hand. "I can't tell. It's a secret."

"You can't keep secrets from me, Sam. I'm your mother."

"She was safe with her great-aunt, Kirsten." It was Phil, coming up behind Syl.

"I didn't know she was with her, Uncle Phil."

"Well, it sounds like that's your mother-in-law's fault. Were you looking for Sam? Were you worried about her?"

"No, I just wondered where she was."

"And I'm sure Angela would have told you if she knew that." Phil glanced over at Angela.

Angela paused for a second. "Sure I would have," she said quietly.

"Then, let's leave it at that. Problem solved." Phil sauntered over to the makeshift bar.

At virtually the same moment, Claire walked into the tent wearing oven mitts and carrying a roasting pan, the smell of dark meat and barbeque sauce wafting behind her. She was followed by Sherry, and then Janet, carrying trays laden with salads and steaming roasted vegetables, respectively. She stopped. "Why is it so quiet in here?" She glanced around. "What happened? What'd I miss?"

"Not a thing," said Phil. "Who wants a beer?"

And the awkward silence went away as the nieces and nephews shouted, "I do!", in quick succession and rushed in Phil's direction.

Syl let go of Sam's hand when Kirsten said something to her daughter about washing up for supper. She followed the two of them out of the tent. "It's not Sam's fault, Kirsten." Kirsten turned sharply and glared at her, her lips in a tight line, then sent Sam on to the house to wash up. Syl watched Sam go in through the back door, then turned her attention back to the young woman in front of her. "I'm sorry. I should have told you I was taking Sam for a walk," she said, "but I was pretty sure Angela would tell you, as we had a few words in the house earlier about Sam's art."

"Yes, you should have told me or, more correctly, *asked* me." Syl felt Kirsten's spit on her bare arm. "And as far as the art is concerned, I've got higher hopes for Sam. I don't want her to think she can be an artist, like *you*."

Syl tried to ignore Kirsten's insult and spoke calmly: "She already *is* an artist, Kirsten, and what higher hopes can you have for your daughter than that she follows her heart and does something she loves?"

"It's too hard to make a living at it."

"Anything worth doing is always hard. I did the work and I *do* make a living at my art. Sam is at least as passionate and talented as I was at her age, probably even more."

Kirsten paused, as if looking for the right words, then replied: "I don't want her to rely on a husband to support her for years while she tries to make it."

That caught Syl off guard. She hardly knew Kirsten, and the venom in her voice was not only unjust but hurtful to her, as an artist and a person almost twice her age. It sounded like Angela speaking. She could only imagine what Angela had told Kirsten, but it explained a lot. Other than Sherry, her sisters-in-law had never spent any real time getting to know her or asking her about her life.

Syl struggled to respond unemotionally: "You have been misinformed, Kirsten. A husband did *not* support me. I have always made a living with my art and I contributed equally to the finances of my marriage."

Kirsten's eyes widened slightly. "But there's no guarantee that will happen for Sam."

"There are never any guarantees in life, but her best chance at success is with the support of her family."

"Well, that's not going to happen. I'm not convinced it's the best thing for her. And I'd appreciate it if you'd stop filling her head with it." And with that Kirsten marched away from Syl to join Sam in the house.

Syl stood where she was, there on Claire's manicured pathway, unable to believe what had just taken place. She understood that a lot of people didn't know anything about art and artists, but for a mother to refuse to support and encourage her daughter on something she loves, whatever it may be, however far it goes, was unimaginable.

Syl looked over at the tent. She couldn't fathom getting through the rest of the weekend now. She started for the front of the house, unable to face the prospect of passing Sam in the back bathroom. But then she heard Sherry calling her name, coming up behind her.

"Where are you going, Syl? Supper's ready. Everyone's lined up to eat."

"I've kind of lost my appetite."

"Don't be silly. Everything's fine. Nobody's had a second thought about the whole thing." Sherry glanced around herself, then leaned in and whispered to Syl: "I saw Don having a word with Angela. She's not too happy, but she deserved it."

Syl's mouth twitched. "You always know how to cheer me up, Sherry! But I'm worried about Sam. I see myself in her. She's a talented kid, a real artist, and her mother refuses to acknowledge her potential. If she doesn't get to pursue her passion, she will never be truly happy."

"Unfortunately, Syl," said Sherry, "she's not your daughter. You can't control this. But if what you say is true, then she will not be able to stifle her artist. And one day she will be an adult, and then she can do whatever she wants."

Syl realized the truth in what Sherry said. The formative years were extremely important, but Sherry was right—she couldn't control this. And the artist inside Sam would, indeed, *not* allow her to stop.

...

The next morning, as Syl descended the stairs from the bedroom, she heard loud voices in the living room, and then her own name. "What about Syl?" she asked as she entered the room. A half dozen family members inside suddenly stopped talking. She looked from face to face.

"Is she with *you*?" It was Angela, standing in the centre of the group.

"Is *who* with me?"

"Sam!" said Kirsten as she stepped forward, glaring at Syl. "Is she with you again, Aunt Sylvia?"

"No, I haven't seen her yet. Why? What's happened?" And then everyone was talking at once.

Don walked up to Syl and spoke quietly to her. "No one has seen Sam this morning. She wasn't in bed in the trailer when her mother got up. The whole yard has been searched and we've come up empty."

"Oh," said Syl. "She's not in someone else's trailer, is she? Did you try the tents?"

"Yes, everyone has been looking." Don paused. "Do you have any thoughts, Syl?" From the look on his face, clearly Don thought she did. Her secret place. Syl suddenly realized that he knew about it, which meant that all of her brothers probably did. Her voice croaked a yes in answer to his question.

Don turned and quieted the rest of them in the room.

"I think I know where she is," said Syl. "I'll go and get her."

"I'm coming with you," said Kirsten, challenging Syl to disagree.

"Me too," said Angela, stepping up behind her daughter-in-law.

"Nobody's going anywhere," said Don sternly.

"Syl will go and get her."

"She's *my* daughter!" protested Kirsten.

"She's not lost, Kirsten," he said to his daughter-in-law. "This isn't the city. Syl knows where she is." He glared at Angela. "And if I see *anyone* following her, they'll have me to answer to!" Some in the group looked down at their feet at this. Angela and Kirsten looked from Don to Syl, jaws rigid, not happy but saying nothing.

The north wind was blowing hard when Syl left the house, howling around the farm buildings and picking up the dry dust in the yard, making mini-tornadoes of it. The caraganas rustled and creaked as she hurried along her path in the ditch, and when she turned at the northeast corner she had to lean into it. The heads of the wheat slapped at her thighs as she made her way along the hedgerow, and in the distance she saw the tops of the willow groves waving wildly at her. She was breathing hard when she reached the third grove. She paused, trying to slow her racing heart, not wanting to do what she must do, knowing she'd probably made things worse for Sam by showing her the secret place. She took a deep breath and let it out slowly, then started her crawl into the grove.

Sam sat facing in Syl's direction, on the pillow on the three-legged stool, clipboard in hand, drawing an old doll. It was posed on the spout of the teapot sitting on the tub. So focused was she on the task at hand, she once again failed to notice her great-aunt's arrival. Though it was sheltered from the wind here, the white noise of dry willow leaves sliding across each other filled the space. Syl walked closer to her. "Sam."

Sam glanced up at her. "Hi, Aunty Sylvia!"

"Everyone was looking for you, Sam. They were worried when they couldn't find you."

"I was here in our secret place, drawing."

"I can see that, but you should have let someone know where you were going."

Sam stopped what she was doing and looked at Syl. "But it's a secret."

"You could have told *me*."

"You were still asleep."

"How long have you been here?"

"I don't know. The sun was a little bit up."

"Well, next time you need to leave a note."

"I can't tell them where I am." Sam's brow furrowed.

"No, but you could say it was where I took you yesterday, or something else that doesn't tell them where it is exactly. Sam, you need to tell someone where the secret place is, so if something happens, someone would know where to look. I'm sorry. I should have told you that yesterday. My mom and dad knew where it was."

Sam again looked at Syl, and her eyes teared up. "I can't tell Mom and Dad. They won't let me come here." A tear fell onto her cheek. "*You* know where it is," she said hopefully.

"Yes, but I don't live here. You might be here when I'm not. How about your grandpa?"

"Maybe, but Grandma is the boss of him."

Syl chuckled. "Sometimes she is, but I think in this case Grandpa would be okay. He'd stick up for you." Just as he had stuck up for Syl this morning.

"But sometimes we come here without Grandpa."

"Well, then, how about Uncle Phil? He'll always be here, and you saw how he took our side yesterday."

There were those beautiful dimples again. "Okay!"

"We'll talk to Uncle Phil later. But now we should go back to the house for breakfast."

"A few minutes more? I'm almost finished."

Syl smiled at her. "I think that would be all right."

Sam went back to work. "I think if Mom sees my drawing she'll know I really *am* an artist," she said as she worked her pencil rapidly over the paper.

And then it was Syl's eyes tearing up. She walked toward the trees to wipe the tears away. That's why Sam came here so early, she thought. She wanted to produce something impressive, something that would sway her mom. Syl feared the worst. If she, herself, a successful artist, had not impressed Sam's mom, how would this child, in her innocence, do so?

"I'm done, Aunty Sylvia!"

Syl walked back to Sam. "May I see it?"

"Not yet. I want Mom to see it first." Sam tucked her page inside the other pages of the pad on the clipboard. Syl helped her put everything else back in the tub, and they secured it with the bungee cords and dragged it back over to the protection of the trees.

This time, Sam led the way out of the secret place and along the path to the farmyard. She turned and walked backward for a few steps to face Syl, her dark bangs standing up in the wind.

"Was Mom really mad at me?" she asked.

"I think she was more worried than mad, Sam," Syl replied, "but you should probably say you're sorry for not leaving a note."

"Okay." Sam turned around again. Syl watched the dark ponytail swinging in front of her and hoped that Kirsten had taken the time, since Syl left the house, to calm down. She added to that a prayer Kirsten would also give Sam's drawing the attention it deserved, and a reaction that wouldn't devastate the child.

As they came into the yard and headed to the house, Sam's older brother tore out the front door and down the steps. He yelled at her as he raced around to the back: "Mom's at the trailer. You're s'pposed to go there!"

Sam grabbed Syl's hand. "Will you come with me, Aunty?"

"Sure I will," said Syl, knowing she shouldn't, guessing she wouldn't be welcome, anticipating Kirsten would slam the door in her face. But she wouldn't abandon Sam now. Especially now. "In for a penny, in for a pound," she murmured.

They walked past the machine shed to an open park, where Phil had the family trailers parked roughly in a circle. Syl let Sam guide her, stepping around cars and over long electrical cords feeding power to everything. She waved at Sherry's twins and their fiancés, standing in front of a couple of blue nylon tents, holding coffee mugs.

And then she spotted Kirsten sitting in front of her trailer across the other side of the circle. Syl's dread increased as she and Sam walked toward her, though she realized how ridiculous that would seem to anyone if they knew it. She was a mature, independent, successful woman. But she was walking in Sam's shoes now, all the years of taunting and teasing she herself had endured now filling them. Because she was different. Because she didn't want to play games or go to parties. Because she took art classes.

Kirsten rose from her chair as they approached, and she went to Sam for a hug. "I'm happy you're back, Sam," she said in a scarily calm voice. She glanced at Syl and led the way to the trailer. "Come in, both of you." Syl looked down at Sam, who had resumed a tight grip on her great-aunt's hand. Even *she* was thrown by her mother's tone.

When they entered the trailer, they found Sam's dad sitting on the bench seat at the table.

Kirsten sat next to him and gestured for Syl and Sam to sit across from them.

"Are you mad at me, Mom?" said Sam.

"Only a little, Sam. I was scared when I couldn't find you. I have to know where you are. You know that, don't you?"

"I'm sorry, Mom. I forgot to leave you a note." Sam glanced up at Syl. "But Aunty Sylvia knew where I was."

"The same place you were yesterday?"

"Yeah, it's a good place to draw."

"Sam—"

"Look, Mom, I drew something for you!" Sam put the clipboard on the table and fanned the sheets to find where she had so carefully hidden her drawing.

"But, Sam—"

"Just look at it, Kirsten," said Syl.

"Aunt Sylvia," said Kirsten, "I explained to you I don't want her to . . . waste . . . her . . . time." Sam had put the drawing in Kirsten's hands, and her mom and dad were now staring at it. They looked at each other and then at Syl, then back to the drawing. Kirsten's mouth fell open and her body softened. "Sam," she said, her voice trembling slightly, "it's beautiful."

Syl quietly let out a breath she didn't realize she was holding and looked down at Sam, who was beaming up at her, eyes bright, dimples huge. She was bouncing a little in her seat, hardly able to contain her excitement.

"Have you never seen her work before?" asked Syl of the couple across the table.

"No," replied Kirsten. "She never showed it to us." Kirsten looked at her husband and he shook his head in agreement.

"I didn't think it was good enough, Mom," said Sam. "Not until Aunty Sylvia told me."

Kirsten glanced at Syl, now unable to hold eye contact. "Sometimes it just takes one to know one," said Syl. "That's all."

Kirsten leaned over the table to take Sam's hand. "I'm so sorry, Sam. I haven't been paying attention. All kids like to draw. I had no idea you were so good at it."

"Well, I'm an artist, Mom," said Sam as she smiled up at Syl once more.

Her mom and dad laughed. "Yes, Sam, it appears you are," said Kirsten. And Sam, bubbling over, showed her parents the details of her drawing.

Syl rose from the bench seat. She was sure

she'd start crying if she stayed, her heart was so near bursting with joy. "I'll see you at breakfast," she said, and she left the young family alone. She headed for the big white tent, her feet barely touching the ground.

As she approached the front of the house, Phil came around the corner of the cotoneaster hedge. "There you are," he said. "I was looking for you."

"I went with Sam to see her parents."

"How'd it go?"

"Well, with everything I tried to do to convince Kirsten of Sam's talent, it was Sam herself who figured it out."

"Really?"

"Yeah. She drew something for her mom."

"It's good?"

"I'm sure it is. I haven't had a chance to see it close up yet, but judging by the reaction of her parents, it's great. And that's all that matters." Syl put her arm through her brother's and they walked toward the white tent. Then she stopped him. "By the way, I get the distinct impression my brothers know about my secret place."

Phil grinned at her. "Yeah, we do. We've always known about it. Mom told us."

"Mom!"

"Yeah, but it was because she wanted to keep your secret. She told us she would tan our hides if we ever followed you or looked for you."

Syl chuckled. "So you knew it existed, but you didn't know where it was."

"No."

"You still don't? None of you?"

"No."

Syl searched her brother's grey eyes and knew he was telling the truth. "Well, I'm going to tell you where it is *now*, because I have this feeling our little grand-niece Sam is going to need you."

End of the Road

Jill's heart pounded painfully in her chest, and each desperate breath of hot dusty air hurt like hell. Muscles in every part of her body ached— calves thighs, back, neck. Even the muscles of her face hurt; she'd been squinting into the sun for the last ten miles. Her hands were throbbing and she couldn't feel her toes anymore. And now the road was rising. Another hill.

She had reached her breaking point.

She shifted her gaze from the white line on the road's shoulder to the speck that was Lloyd, now at the crest of the hill. Only a glint of sunlight on his rear fender told her it was him. He was doing it again, she thought incredulously. "Lloyd!" she screamed with what breath she had left, knowing full well he couldn't hear her. "Wait up!"

She sat up and stinging salty sweat ran into her eyes. She blinked furiously and stopped pedalling. The momentum of her bicycle carried her only a few more feet on the inclined pavement. She was crazy to stop on a hill, she knew that, but she had to. She had to get her itchy helmet off, she had to wet her parched throat, she had to let sensation tingle its way back into her fingers and toes. She had to put her body vertical.

She freed both feet from the clipless pedals and touched the right one to the ground as the bike came to a stop. She gasped as she put her weight on the foot and dismounted. Now relieved of more than an hour of unrelenting pressure, the nerves in her behind told her how sore she really was. "How am I going to get back on this thing?" she wondered aloud.

She gently lowered her bike, which was laden with camping gear, onto the gravel shoulder of the road and then stood, arching her back in relief, and surveyed her surroundings. Rolling prairie stretched as far as she could see. On her side of the highway, dark earth lay fallow, puffs of precious soil whirling upwards to be blown to some needless place. Swallows swooped angrily over it, dive bombing a sparrow hawk that had intruded on their space in search of an easy meal. On the opposite side were endless waving grasses, withered in the August heat.

A gopher stood frozen on its haunches a few feet away, watching her. "Who the heck picked this paradise?" she asked it, and the gopher scurried into its hole. Jill knew the answer: Lloyd did. He always did. "Why do I go along with these things?" she cried. There was no reply. A light breeze played with the tendrils of red hair escaped from her ponytail.

Jill took a long drink from her water bottle. All she could taste was dust. The mid-afternoon sun beat down on the top of her bare head and her blue tank top was pasted to her back. She pulled sun block out of her handlebar bag and applied it to her pink arms and legs, over the salt and grime already caked there. Then, looking first up, then down the highway, she made her way into the taller grasses in the bottom of the ditch, pulled down her shorts, and squatted. "This is what I'm reduced to," she said to the gopher, which had emerged once again from its hole, "peein' in the ditch."

She climbed back up to the roadside and looked wearily at her bike, lying there like a grotesquely-burdened pack mule unable to get up. Her eyes fell on "the soft, comfortable seat, designed especially for the wider female pelvis." Yeah, she thought, wincing, I'm feeling every inch of my wider female pelvis at the moment, thank you very much. She glanced up the hill, but the speck had already disappeared.

She sighed. Lloyd was playing a mind game with her. And he was winning—she was frustrated as hell. It was not so much that he show her he could go farther faster, though that was part of it. No, the main thing was that he show her he wasn't going to slow up for her, especially since she had asked him to, again and again.

"But I'm not going too fast," he had protested when she finally caught up to him at his last rest spot. "It's just the right pace for me. I can't help it. Why don't you try pedalling a little faster?"

"I'm pedalling as fast as I can," Jill said defensively. "And *I* can't help it—it's just the right pace for *me*!"

"But you expect *me* to pull back?" he asked.

"I thought the whole idea of these trips was that we get away and spend time together. How are we accomplishing that if you're always so far ahead of me, and I have to work twice as hard just to get within shouting distance of you? What if something should happen? You don't even bother looking back to see if I'm still coming!"

"Nothing's going to happen," he scoffed.

It was no use. As always, he couldn't see her

point of view. She'd fooled herself once more into thinking that her husband really wanted her to be with him, when in fact she was probably along just to do the packing and unpacking. And the cooking, of course. The only positive was that it was only a half-day's ride from home and only one night camping. They'd be home tomorrow.

Jill was suddenly jerked back to the present by the screech of tires and a cloud of choking exhaust fumes and dust. A vehicle was stopping. It slid onto the gravel shoulder ahead of her bike, then swerved wildly to avoid the ditch. She could just make out a badly-rusted, faded-orange pickup as the cloud settled. Then the engine died and the truck's two doors opened.

From the driver's side emerged a man as large as he was filthy. Even from twenty feet away Jill could see the stains of countless greasy meals on what had once been a white T-shirt. The shirt was stretched over an enormous beer belly that poured over and obscured the top of his baggy blue jeans. He was caked from the knees down with God knows what. He wore a black ball cap, and a package of cigarettes was rolled up in one short sleeve, James Dean style. Long, blond hair stuck out in frizzy disarray from beneath the cap, and the same mess obscured most of his face and neck.

"Well, Les," the man called loudly as he walked slowly toward the back of the truck, "what have we got *here*?" His left hand ran along the top edge of the box, and his right hand flicked the remains of a still-burning cigarette onto the asphalt.

Jill's heart quickened and she was suddenly bathed in sweat again. A bittersweet odour of salt and sunblock assailed her nostrils. She watched them approach through the settling dust.

"Looks like the little lady's all alone, Jimmy," replied the man who had climbed out of the passenger side. Les was emaciated compared to Jimmy. Another filthy, used-to-be-white T-shirt hung on a skeletal frame, and tattered blue jeans were covered with the same unidentifiable muck. Stringy, dark hair framed a deathly-pale face. He carried a half-empty bottle of dark liquid in one hand. Then he stumbled and fell, landing on his hands and knees. The bottle shattered. He didn't move for a few seconds, then rose laboriously to his feet and stared, disbelieving, at the bottle's neck still in his hand. "Sheeeit!"

Jimmy looked over at him, and then calmly

turned to Jill and said, "Maybe the little lady can make it up to you, Les."

"Yeah," Les replied, looking Jill up and down, "maybe she can." He tossed the remains of his bottle into the ditch.

"What's the worst that could happen?" Lloyd had asked her. "You might blow a tire, but you know how to fix that. You have everything you need with you."

"I'm not worried about a tire, Lloyd," she explained. "What if some nut case comes along? I'm all alone back there."

"It's not going to happen, Jill," he insisted. "This is Saskatchewan!"

Well, Saskatchewan wasn't what it used to be, Lloyd, she thought as Les and Jimmy came toward her. They didn't seem to be in much of a hurry, but it would only be seconds before they covered the ground between the truck and her. As they advanced, their jackal grins grew. Jimmy's eyes almost disappeared into his fat face, which was flushed pink with the heat.

She wanted to run, but her feet were suddenly rooted in the soft gravel. She wanted to scream, but her parched throat denied her voice. She looked up the hill behind the two men, but Lloyd was nowhere in sight. Les was now close enough that she could see his bloodshot eyes, rimmed with dark circles.

Then a tiny rivulet of sweat formed on her face. Droplets gathered and ran together, sidestepped the dirt, accelerated in a line at her mouth, and reached her chin. As more droplets gathered there, a drop formed and grew, heavier and heavier, until it hung precariously. Then it let go, cooling slightly as it fell, and landed on her chest. And it loosened the stranglehold of fear. Jill jumped reflexively and, without hesitation, turned and leapt into the ditch.

"Hey!" the two men shouted simultaneously.

"Bitch!" yelled Les. "Where the hell d'ya think yer going?"

Jill scrambled the short distance to the bottom and then scrambled up the other side, heading to the dark field. But Les was right behind her. She could smell the booze and hear him grunting in his effort, and just as she reached the top, he grabbed her left ankle. She turned onto her back and glanced down at him grinning up at her.

"Gotcha!"

"Let go of me!" she screamed at him, and she kicked at his scrawny hand with her free foot.

But he held on. And Jimmy was on his way, breathing hard as he waded through the knee-high grasses at the bottom, his face beet red from the exertion. She looked frantically around herself, desperate for anything she might use as a weapon. Then she glanced over her head to the edge of the field.

Without hesitation she twisted her body until she was on her belly, bruising her own ankle as Les tightened his grip. She pushed her free foot against the upslope and, bracing herself with her left hand, reached up into the grasses with her right. She stretched, pulling the muscles in her side until they could give no more, stretched until she broke through to the field.

Then she scooped up the dark earth into a tight fist, whirled around to her assailant, and threw the dirt into his face. Les screeched and let go, and she climbed quickly out of the ditch and into the field, ignoring the profanity that continued out of the two men's mouths. She gained a foothold in the soft dirt and ran, hard.

But they didn't follow. She dared a glance over her shoulder after several seconds, sure that they would be in hot pursuit. Instead, they were clambering up onto the road. She stopped, and the two looked at her from across the ditch.

"Next time!" screamed Les.

No. Not next time. There'd be no next time.

The two men started back to the pickup, still yelling obscenities at her, and then Les stumbled again. Only this time he had tripped on something. Her bike. Her heart lurched when the two of them bent over it, and she held her breath as she saw the contents of her panniers being tossed into the ditch, hoping they wouldn't find her wallet. But Jimmy rose a few moments later, waving it at her, mocking her with it, hooting and yelling, saving face after he and his buddy had blundered their attempt to assault her. She felt a nauseating disgust in the back of her throat as the two sauntered back to their truck, playing the victors. They climbed in and the old orange pickup came to life. It roared off the shoulder of the road, sending a shower of pebbles in its wake, and headed up the hill.

The prairie fell silent again. The swallows had given up and the lone sparrow hawk glided unimpeded over the field. Jill walked back to the highway. Her two-wheeled mule was still lying on its side, but its guts were spilled out—plastic cups and plates, matches, frying pan. Her sleeping bag lay in a heap and the toilet paper had unrolled into the ditch. But the bike itself was fine.

And she was fine. Without Lloyd.

Lloyd. She looked to the top of the hill, almost indistinguishable now in the shimmering heat, and wondered when the orange pickup would catch him.

Twenty minutes passed before she had gathered up the scattered contents of her panniers and repacked them. There was one way, and one way only, that her gear fit on her bike. She'd learned that early on. When it was done she put her helmet back on, refastened her gloves, and pulled her bike upright. She raised her right leg over the seat, snapped her right shoe into its pedal and pushed off, then snapped her left shoe into its pedal. She took a deep breath and set her tender bottom gingerly onto the seat.

And then she coasted to the bottom of the hill and headed home.

Irish Eyes

Colleen stepped, dripping, through the door between the women's shower room and the swimming pool room and immediately noticed something wrong with the lighting. She looked up and saw that every other row of long fluorescent lights in the ceiling was unlit. Probably another cost-saving measure by Tony, she thought. The owner of the fitness club. He had stopped providing towels a few months ago, then it was shampoo in the shower, now this. As she slipped into the water she noticed that the reduced lighting made the chipped, yellow paint at the bottom of the pool look even dirtier than usual. Today the water was also a little too warm, bathtub-like, and she tried not to think about what Tony was trying to kill with the extra dose of chlorine her nose detected.

The fitness club was old and run down, but a neighbour she had spoken to a few weeks ago had heard a rumour it was sold. She hoped the rumour was true and that the new owner would not only keep it operating but fix the place up. She dreaded the idea of having to drive to the huge public complex, the only other place in town with an indoor pool, and fight with other swimmers for space to do her laps. At this time of day, after the early-morning rush, she had this small pool to herself, which was how she liked it. It was one of the reasons she continued to come here. The other was that it was only three blocks from her house.

Colleen lowered herself into the water and adjusted her swim goggles over her eyes. She took a breath and dipped her head below the surface, then pushed off with her feet and began her journey along the giant blue dashed line beneath her. She focused on the movements of her arms and legs, the rolling of her body, and the bubbles boiling past her ears, and she soon relaxed into the rhythm, her mind clearing of the tasks she had waiting for her when she arrived at work in a couple of hours.

She did a vigorous front crawl for ten laps and switched to breast stroke. It was then, as she faced forward down the length of the pool, that she saw him. A man was watching her from the other side of the glass window between the pool room and the club's reception area. The reflection of the lights on the glass, and the veil of water on her goggles, prevented her from capturing any details, but there was no missing his full dark beard and moustache. She turned and did another lap, but as she made the return trip, he walked away. The light in the reception area reflected off a full head of short dark hair to go with his beard.

She stopped when she reached the end of the pool, some twenty feet from the glass. She raised her goggles and waited, but he didn't return. Ordinarily, she wouldn't concern herself, but the window was behind the reception desk and wasn't for public use. The receptionist, usually Tony's mother, Sophia, would glance in to be sure she was all right, given that she swam alone, but she was the only person Colleen ever saw at that window, and she'd been swimming here for three years. She went back to her swim but found herself checking the window with every return length.

By the time she had finished her laps, showered, and dressed, Colleen had dismissed the uneasy feeling the man at the window had caused her. She had reasoned that he must know Tony and Sophia to have been behind the reception desk, and he was just killing time watching her swim. She threw her wet things into her gym bag and left the locker room, passing the reception desk on her way to the front door. Sophia called out to her as she did every day: "See you tomorrow, Colleen!" Colleen answered her in kind.

As she walked across the parking lot, she ruffled her short, blond hair with her hands, the better to let the warm summer breeze finish drying it for her, then reached for her sunglasses in the outside pocket of her gym bag. She didn't notice a man get out of a car and walk toward her, and he was almost upon her when he called out her name. She jumped, and a sharp "Oh!" leapt from her throat.

"Colleen?" he said again as she turned and stopped. She looked up into the face of a tall man with short, dark hair and a substantial beard and moustache.

"You were inside watching me swim, weren't you?" she said accusingly, taking a few steps back and holding her bag protectively in front of her.

"Sorry, I didn't mean to scare—"

"How do you know me?" she demanded.

"Colleen, it's me, Sean."

She frowned, still suspicious of him. "I don't know any Seans."

"Yes you do. Sean Sullivan, from high school. St. Thomas, class of 1991?"

She peered at him. That *was* her school and her graduating year, but there were lots of students in that class, and that was more than twenty-five years ago and two provinces away. She didn't recognize him, but who *could* with all that facial hair? And then she looked into his eyes—they were a startling blue—and two words suddenly popped into her head: Irish eyes. His name didn't mean anything to her, but somehow she remembered his eyes. "Sean? I can't believe it! What are you doing here?"

He smiled and crows' feet appeared around his eyes. "I live here now, arrived yesterday, in fact." He glanced back to the fitness club. "I just finished my workout. I *thought* I recognized you in the pool."

"Good heavens, how?"

"I was on the boys' swim team in high school, remember? The girls' team always had the pool first, so I had lots of opportunity to watch you swim. I recognized your style."

He recognized her *style* after all these years? Colleen looked at him again, trying to line up the faces of the boys' team in her head, but she could only see one of them: Rick, the boy she dated in grades eleven and twelve. All the others were a blur. "Oh yeah!" she said as if she remembered him, assuming a little white lie couldn't hurt anything. She would pull out her high school yearbooks and refresh her memory of Sean Sullivan when she got home. "So, did you move into this neighbourhood?" she asked.

"Yup." He turned around and pointed to the club owner's residence sitting on the two-acre property, a stone's throw away from the club itself. "Right there."

"You're kidding! *You* bought the club?"

"Yup again."

"I'm impressed!"

"Well, I got a pretty good deal. The place isn't in great shape, and I'm going to have to pour a lot of money into it."

"I'm so glad you will keep it going. And fix it up. I swim here pretty much daily."

"Then I guess we'll see a lot of each other."

"I guess so. When are you moving in?"

"I'm here a week early to come up to speed on operations before the handover, but my stuff doesn't arrive for a couple of months. I'm staying with a friend while I have the house renovated.

It's in almost as bad a shape as the club, but I like the idea of living on site, so I'm going to fix it up."

"And your family will arrive later, too?"

"No family. I'm divorced, about five years ago. And we had no kids. You?"

"No husband, no kids. Career girl, I guess. Never found someone who would follow me to the ends of the earth." Sean's eyebrows rose quizzically. She explained: "I'm in banking. I moved around a lot, getting new branches up and running in places where they were needed, which generally meant smaller towns on the prairies. I did that for twenty years, until they gave me my own branch to manage here, and then I was finally able to set down roots. That was about three years ago."

"Good for you! I've been watching for an opportunity on the west coast for a while now. Wanted to get away from the prairie winter." He looked at his watch. "Hey, would you like to continue this conversation over coffee? I have some time, and I passed a Tim Horton's on the way here this morning."

"I'm sorry, I can't. I've got to get home and get changed, then get to work. I usually do the late shift so I can swim in the morning."

"Well, I hope we can catch up soon."

"Yeah, let's do that after you're settled in."

"You look great, Colleen," he said as he backed away, and then he turned to go to his car.

"You too, Sean," she called out to him, even though she couldn't remember his high school face at all.

And with that Colleen threw her gym bag over her shoulder and started home, her head spinning. She just had a personal conversation with a guy she couldn't remember, like they were old friends. The only thing she truly remembered was his eyes. Irish eyes? Where did *that* come from. Something nagged at her, but she couldn't put her finger on it. "Thank heavens you kept your yearbooks, Colleen," she muttered out loud. She hoped something in them would prompt a clearer memory of him.

It wasn't until that evening after work that she had a chance to pull the yearbook from her graduating year off the shelf in her den. She found Sean Sullivan's picture easily, as the photos were arranged alphabetically, but she was surprised by his face. "Huh," she said aloud. The man she talked to this morning was *this* guy? She recognized the boy in the photo, she even vaguely remembered him in some of her classes, but she didn't really *know* him. He didn't belong to her circle of friends, and she wasn't sure they'd even said two words to each other in the four years they were at St. Thomas together. She shrugged. There were two hundred students in her class; she didn't know a *lot* of them. She looked for pictures of the boys' swim team, too. Sure enough, there he was in the photo of the team, standing almost a head above the other boys, including her old boyfriend. But the photo didn't help her remember anything about Sean, including that he swam with Rick. She pulled out all her yearbooks and looked through all the pictures this time, looking for Sean but also anything else that might jog her memory of him. But she was unsuccessful. He was just a face in a crowd at a large high school.

She sat back in her chair. It was surprising that Sean remembered her, and even more surprising that he spoke to her, given they didn't really know each other in high school. But they were adults now. All that crazy high school stuff was behind them. She turned forty-five this year; he probably did the same. You can start a conversation with someone you shared a high school with when you're forty-five, even if you couldn't when you were sixteen.

Suddenly something nudged her memory. She tried to grab hold of it, bring it into her consciousness, but it hovered, ghost-like, at the edges. The ghost whispered "Irish eyes" to her again, but when she tried to place the startling blue eyes she saw this morning onto the black-and-white face in the yearbook, she could not give the ghost form. If there was something significant to remember about Sean, it was eluding her. She shrugged to herself. It really didn't matter. She didn't know him *then*, but she could get to know him *now*. He seemed like a nice guy.

...

After the handover week at the club, Colleen noticed tradespeople coming and going from Sean's house, but she rarely saw him on the property. She was only there an hour or so in the morning, so she didn't really *expect* to see him, though they had waved to each other a few times. No renovations on the club *per se* yet, but there was a young man and young woman working at the reception desk who were new, fit and enviably muscled, a living advertisement for the club in their athletic attire. Towels were again provided, cleanliness in the locker room and pool area had significantly improved, and the pool temperature and chlorine levels were more comfortable now. That's all she really cared about. Sean was clearly on the right path.

One morning, about six weeks later, there were no more trucks and vans parked at the house, and Sean was standing in front, stroking his beard, admiring the new exterior paint job, a desert-sand colour with slightly darker trim around the new windows. She wandered over to him. "Looks great, Sean," she said.

"You like it?"

"I do. A nice contrast to the fir trees behind it, yet warm and earthy."

"That's what I was going for—earthy." He grinned at her.

She smirked at him. "You're teasing me, aren't you?" she said.

"Just a little. Do you have time to see the inside?"

"Sure! I happen to have today off. No need to rush home."

"I don't worry about days off. I have a come-and-go policy with my staff. They never know when to expect me. It keeps them on their toes."

"Nice to own your own business!"

"Always have, always will."

"Really?"

"How about I show you the house and then take you for coffee. I'll tell you all about it."

"Sounds great!"

Colleen was impressed with the renovations Sean had made to the house. Though she'd never seen the inside of it before, she was pretty sure the more-than-thirty-years-old two-storey didn't have an open concept great room, gas fireplace, and modern kitchen before. The three bedrooms upstairs became a master bedroom with a large ensuite, as well as a spare bedroom. The bathrooms on both floors were completely redone. The rusts and tans and golds on the walls made the place feel warm and welcoming, even without furniture in the place. "It's really beautiful, Sean," she said to him as she preceded him down the stairs to the front door. "I love the colour scheme you chose." She glanced over her shoulder at him and they said "Earthy!" at the same time and laughed together.

Half an hour later they were settled in at Tim Horton's, each with a cup of the brew and, Sean insisted, a blueberry muffin. Colleen was amazed to learn that Sean had a head for numbers, just as she did, but had been a financial planner in their home town on the prairies for twenty-five years, the last twenty as owner of his own firm. After his divorce, he decided to get out of the business and look for something completely different and less stressful. A place people were happy to come to, he said. Hence the fitness club.

"Are you still swimming?" Colleen asked when they had finished filling each other in on their professional history.

"No, not since high school. I got into running instead. It didn't require a building to be open at odd hours, and I worked a *lot* of odd hours. I had equipment at home to do my workout and was often running outside in the dark. But I liked it; it was quiet on the streets at night."

"And now you have all the equipment you need and flexible work hours."

"And a pool that can be open whenever I want it to be."

"So, you're thinking of swimming again?"

"I thought I'd give it a try."

"Just remember the cardinal rule." She wagged her finger at him. "Never swim alone."

Sean stroked his beard. "Hmmm, I wonder who I could swim with." He looked past her, as if someone sitting behind her would have the answer." Then he grinned at her.

"Well, I kinda like the pool to myself," she teased, "but I guess there's room for one more, if the owner wants to swim with the likes of me!"

"I don't know if my swimming will measure up to the likes of you after all these years," he said.

She chuckled. "Oh, I think with a little hard work you'll be able to keep up."

Colleen could feel her face flushing. Were they seriously *flirting* with each other? Forty-five years old and she felt like she was back in high school again.

"Colleen?" said Sean.

"Oh, sorry. The hallways of St. Thomas suddenly flashed before my eyes."

"Yeah, running into you has brought back some memories for me, too, in the last few weeks."

"Good ones?"

"Some. Mostly I couldn't wait for high school to be over."

"Me, too."

"Really? You seemed to be very popular. You

had a lot of friends."

"Yeah, but none of them were *close* friends. We didn't keep in touch after graduation."

"Not even with Rick?" Sean looked down at his cup, his left forefinger tapping on the mug.

He remembered she dated Rick? "Only for that summer after graduation. Then I went to university. He didn't."

"I knew you were smart. I could never understand why you were with Rick." He looked back up at her. "Except I guess the prettiest girl in the school always dates the prettiest boy."

"I wasn't the pretti—"

"*I* thought you were."

Colleen could feel the colour rise to her cheeks again.

Sean quickly said, "I didn't mean to embarrass you."

She patted her cheeks. "That's okay. I...I suddenly feel like a teenager again!"

He chuckled. "To be honest, so do I!"

Colleen laughed and took a drink of her coffee. Had Sean just admitted he'd had a crush on her in high school? She'd had no idea. But how could she? She didn't know him back then.

And there it was again—Irish eyes. Suddenly

the ghost was back and was starting to take form. She struggled to see it, but then it disappeared.

"You're Irish, aren't you?" she blurted out.

Suddenly the smile on Sean's face faltered. He paused. "Yeah, I guess so. My great-grandparents came from Ireland. Why do you ask?" The crows' feet had slackened, and the tone of his voice had flattened.

Something was wrong. Colleen tried to think quickly. "Oh, uh no reason, really. You have stunning blue eyes, and your name, I uh, suddenly remembered something I learned in biology class all those years ago: dark hair and blue eyes are common in the Irish." She fumbled for her lip balm in her bag, praying he hadn't been in her biology class. She had just made that stuff up.

There was a short, awkward silence. "Well," said Sean, pushing his chair away from the table, and abruptly ending it. "I should get back to the club. I have some bookwork to do." He drained his coffee mug and put it on top of his plate. "Can I drop you at home?"

"No, the club is okay. I need a little walk after that muffin, which was delicious by the way, thank you." She couldn't look at him.

"You're welcome. We'll do it again."

She looked up from her chair. His big smile was suddenly back. "I'll buy next time," she said.

"Well, okay," he said, gesturing for her to go ahead of him.

When Colleen got home, the first thing she did was get onto her laptop and "Google" "Irish eyes." She sighed in relief when she found what she was looking for: dark hair and blue eyes *were* common in Ireland, at least before people from other countries began to mix with them, more than 2000 years ago. "Phew," she said aloud as she sat back in her chair. "I'm okay, just in case he looks it up."

Maybe she *did* learn that in biology class, but she didn't remember. She had been about to tell Sean about the words "Irish eyes" floating around in her head since they first encountered each other, find out if it meant anything to him, but something about mentioning the word "Irish" had initially caused a reaction in him, and she had to quickly think of something else to say. She thought she had lost him but, thankfully, he quickly recovered his good humour. She wasn't quite sure what had happened, but she wasn't going to mention "Irish" to him ever again. She was enjoying getting to know him and thought there might be something more that could develop between them. Part of her wished she had known the boy in high school who had thought she was the prettiest girl.

...

A few days later Sean's moving truck was sitting at his house when she arrived for her swim. She didn't see him for several days after that, and then a week later she arrived to find a notice on the door of the women's locker room. It announced the closure of the pool in two weeks for renovations. She carried on into the locker room and got changed for her swim, happy he was taking care of the pool first.

As Colleen sat on the edge of the pool, adjusting her goggles onto her face, she heard a door open. Someone had exited the men's shower room. "Oh, no," she muttered to herself. She wasn't going to have the pool to herself this morning. She raised her goggles to get a better look at who it was and was surprised to see it was Sean. The sight of him in a swimmer's suit made her heart flutter. For a man in his mid-forties, he was very lean and muscular. At this particular moment, wet in a tight swimmer's suit, no makeup, lots of bare skin showing, she was glad she could say much the same for herself.

She waited for him to make his way to her at the end of the pool and sit down on her right. "You decided to join me, finally?" she said.

"Today's the day!" He placed his goggles over his eyes and grinned at her. "You ready?"

"That *thing*," she said pointing at his beard, which was still dripping from his shower, "is going to slow you down."

He stroked the beard. "We'll see." He used his arms to hoist himself into the pool, then submerged and pushed off with his feet.

"Yes, we will!" she said, more than up for the challenge.

But they didn't race. They swam at the same pace, side by side, just a few feet from each other. It was nice, thought Colleen. Intimate. Fifty laps later, they were sitting together again at the edge of the pool. "I can't believe you did all those laps without stopping, considering you haven't been swimming in more than twenty-five years!" she said. "I'm impressed!"

"Well, I have a confession to make," Sean replied. "I've been swimming at night since we talked about it."

"What? That's cheating!" she said. "And you broke the cardinal rule by swimming alone."

"I'm sorry, but my ego wouldn't let me look bad to you. And I wanted to swim *with* you, not be stopping and starting, alone."

"Well, I enjoyed our swim, together."

"So did I. I'll try to join you whenever I can, if that's okay with you."

"I'd like that."

Somehow, given all the workmen coming and going to the club, Sean managed to join her several more times before the pool was closed. Colleen found herself watching the door to the men's shower room, waiting for him, disappointed if he didn't show. Though they didn't talk much on their swimming mornings together, they continued to swim side by side and challenged each other with gradually increasing speed. She looked so forward to it, she wondered how badly she would miss it when it stopped while the pool was closed. It scared her a bit. She hadn't known him for very long, but she was pretty sure she had already fallen for him. She hadn't been able to take him out for coffee yet, he was so busy with the renovations, and once the pool was closed she had no reason to come to the club at all. She didn't want to lose their connection, but she also didn't want to look like a stalker, dropping in for no reason than to catch sight of him. She considered buying a full club membership so she'd have a valid excuse.

But then, sitting on the edge of the pool together, after a long swim on the last day the pool was open, Sean asked her to his house for dinner that same night.

Her heart soared. "I'd love to," she said.

"I've finally got everything unpacked and in its place," he said.

"I look forward to seeing it," she said.

"I hope you look forward to more than just seeing the house," he teased.

She looked into his sparkling blue eyes. "Is this a proper date, then?"

"Is that all right?"

She put her wet hand over his, where it lay curved over the edge of the pool. "It's more than all right."

He leaned toward her. "And how about we get the first kiss out of the way?"

"Here? Now?"

"Yes, here and now. Then there will be no awkwardness tonight."

"But we're both sopping wet, our hair dripping into our eyes. It's not very romantic."

"Sure it is. I'm showing you I will kiss you even at your worst."

"This isn't my worst, believe—"

"Shhh," he said. And he planted a sweet, soft kiss on her lips, lingering just long enough to make her spine tingle.

And then he got to his feet and headed to the men's locker room, leaving her savouring the moment. He turned back when he got to the door and called to her. "I'm barbequing," he said. "You like salmon, I hope!"

"Love it!"

"Seven o'clock—don't be late!"

...

Colleen arrived exactly at 7 p.m., dressed in a flowery, sleeveless summer dress with a swishy skirt to just above her knees, flip-flops on her feet. Sean opened the door in a T-shirt over long cargo shorts, bare feet. She handed him a bottle of Pinot Grigio she had bought on her last visit to her favourite local estate winery. He took it from her and ushered her in, then leaned in and kissed her gently on the cheek, causing the hairs to rise on her arms. She slipped off her flip-flops and followed him across the dark plank floor in the direction of the kitchen, stopping to admire his beautiful great room, now appointed with tan leather couch and chairs, and solid-wood end tables arranged around a contemporary shag rug. Abstract paintings of various sizes brought all kinds of colour and interest to the room. "Is all the art from the same artist?"

Sean pulled the cork out of the Pinot and began pouring it. "Good eye! Yes, in here it is."

"They're beautiful," said Colleen as she walked toward one. "It says 'Diana' on the bottom right corner. Diana who?"

"Diana Sullivan. My ex-wife."

"Really! She's very good."

"I know. I love her stuff. That's why I asked for what we had hanging in our house in the divorce agreement."

"She didn't mind?"

"No. It was a pretty amicable separation."

"What went wrong, if you don't mind my asking?"

"I'm a money guy. She's an artist. Didn't have a lot in common, I guess."

"Opposites usually attract, don't they?"

"That's what they say, and we did. But

opposites have trouble living together, in my experience." Sean walked over to where she was, standing at the fireplace, and handed her a glass of wine. He raised his glass to her. "To the opposite of opposites attracting." She smiled at him as they touched glasses, and then they both drank. "Mmm, that's good," he said.

"So you think we're the opposite of opposites?" she asked.

"I think we have quite a lot in common so far," he replied. "We went to the same high school, we were both on the swim teams, we both went into money professions." He paused, thinking. "Ah, yes. We both like salmon!"

Colleen chucked. "You don't think it'll be too boring with so much in common?"

"We haven't gotten to know each other personally very well yet. Maybe there will be *something* we can disagree on."

She laughed. "We can only hope!"

And so their evening of getting to know each other began. She sat at a wooden table set on a lovely stone patio that Sean had put in at the back of the house. She watched him put a thick salmon filet on a cedar plank on the barbeque, followed by a vegetable medley to stir fry on the side burner. They sipped their wine and chatted while he cooked, and they talked. About family, the travel they'd done, even art.

Colleen helped Sean clean up the dishes after the delicious meal, and he brought decaf coffees with Grand Marnier to the patio, where they sat next to each other in cushioned Adirondacks in front of a fire bowl. They were quiet for a while, mesmerized by the flames, and Colleen wondered if he was thinking, as she was, how lucky they were to find each other after all these years. She couldn't help but wonder again about what her life may have been like had she fallen for Sean in high school.

And then Sean took her coffee mug from her, leaned forward, and set both mugs on the rim of the concrete bowl. He rose, held out his hand to her and she stood, and he drew her close. "I hope it's not too soon to say so," he said to her, "but I think I've fallen for you." His eyes held hers.

Her heart swelled. "Me too," she said.

"I never thought I'd get another chance to say it."

"Another chance?"

"The first time was in high school, but I couldn't get near you." And then he lowered his head and they kissed, passionately and longingly, like they had been looking for each other all their lives. And when Sean took her hand and led her inside and up the stairs to his bedroom, she didn't hesitate to follow.

Colleen woke early the next morning with a start, her heart racing from a bad dream. It was light in the room, and she was on her side, turned away from Sean. She turned onto her back and blinked at the ceiling, not wanting to fall back asleep. Sean was still asleep on his back beside her, thick lashes lying peacefully on his cheeks, his beard in disarray. She breathed deeply to slow her heart and tried to vanquish the dream. She was losing parts of it already, but she knew she would never forget the ending. It had been a weird dream, bits of the past and present mixed together, crystal clear at times, a little blurry around the edges at others.

There had been a swimming pool in her dream, not the club's pool but the one at St. Thomas High School. She and Sean, as they were now, in their forties, were in the water. They had the pool to themselves, but they were kissing underwater, like she'd seen in the movies. Then suddenly other people's legs plunged into the pool, and she and Sean quickly rose to the surface. "Hey, Irish!" someone behind her yelled. She turned and saw that it was Rick, her old boyfriend, but the Rick of high school, sixteen years old. The others, four of them, she knew were his buddies from the swim team, though she couldn't see their faces. Rick had a wooden baseball bat in his two hands, using it as a buoy as he kicked towards them. "What do you think you're doing, Irish?" he said, his eyes narrow and his mouth tight, as all the boys advanced on them. Colleen tried to scream at him, but nothing would come out of her mouth. Rick's buddies grabbed Sean and moved him to the side of the pool and pinned him there. He wasn't fighting them, and Colleen couldn't understand why, but she couldn't get any sound out of her throat, and she couldn't move to help him. She was immobilized, yet treading water. And then Rick took the baseball bat to Sean's head, again and again, and the blood ran into the water until the entire pool was red. The boys released him and his Irish eyes held hers as his body sunk into the water.

That's when she woke up. *Irish eyes?* It hadn't entered her mind since their coffee at Tim's. Why would it come to her in this horrible dream?

"You look like you've seen a ghost," said Sean, beside her in bed. He'd risen onto his elbow and was looking down at her, worry creasing his forehead.

She turned toward him and wove her hand into his. "Just a bad dream."

He lowered himself to his pillow, facing her. "Do you want to tell me about it?"

"No, it's gone now," she said, but she was lying. This one wouldn't be gone for a while, if ever. She snuggled into his chest, which was almost as hairy as his face.

Sean wrapped his arms around her. "Should I be worried that you had a bad dream after a night of making love with me?" he teased.

"No, not at all!" She lifted her face to his. "I often have intense dreams, sometimes good, sometimes bad, after experiencing intense emotion the night before."

He brought his nose to meet hers and his eyes sparkled at her, his moustache tickling her lips as he smiled. "It *was* kind of intense, wasn't it?"

"Yes, it was," she said, smiling back, her desire for him building inside once more.

"How about a shower?" He nuzzled her neck.

"Together?"

"Of course. Didn't you see the twin rain shower heads and taps?"

She had, and she had hoped he had *her*, alone, in mind when he installed them. She gave him a quick peck on the mouth. "Race ya!"

"Hey, no fair—it's on your side of the bed!"

...

In the weeks that followed that first night, Colleen felt like she spent more nights at Sean's house than her own. She was dizzy with happiness, whether or not they made love or fell into bed and cuddled instead, too tired from work. Sean was overwhelmed with the renovations and trying to keep at least parts of the club open for clients. He didn't want to lose clients to another club by closing altogether, even though the renos might have been completed sooner. Despite the stress he was under, he always made time for her, and left his frustrations at the door. She didn't know such a man existed, and she was in love. Even though it had only been a few months, she was certain that she and Sean would spend the rest of their lives together.

It was after 11 p.m. one evening, while they were still enjoying their decaf coffee after a late dinner at Sean's house, when Sean said to her, "I've got a surprise for you. The pool is done. Just a few last-minute things I had to do. That's why dinner was late."

"Fantastic!" said Colleen. "I can't wait to get back to it and leave the public complex behind. The last four weeks, swimming without you, have *not* been enjoyable."

"How about right now? We'll christen it together."

"Hmmm, a midnight swim. Sounds romantic!" As it happens, my suit's in the car."

"Perfect. Let's do it!"

Twenty minutes later, Colleen sat at their usual spot at the edge of the pool, admiring the renovations. The surface of the pool itself had been repaired and was as smooth as silk, turquoise with white lines on the bottom to guide swimmers. New non-slip decking surrounded the pool and windows, and skylights had been added to bring natural light into the room.

Sean was taking unusually long in the men's room, she thought, and when he finally emerged from the shower room, she could see why. She couldn't believe it—he had shaved off his beard and moustache. "What did you *do*?" she called to him as he walked toward her.

"Surprise!" he called back. "I had this feeling you didn't really like my beard."

"Well, I was getting kind of *used* to it," she said apologetically.

"That's not the same as liking it. But I was getting tired of it myself, so here I am—exposed!"

He sat down next to her, on her right as usual. "I *do* like seeing your face," she said, "though it'll take me a few minutes to adjust, you look so different." She ran her fingers over the left side of his face. "It feels so nice and smooth!"

"And your hand feels so nice on my face," he said and held it there with his left hand. Then he took her hand away and kissed it.

She leaned in and kissed his cheek. "I haven't been able to do *that* properly before."

"So, what do you think of the pool room," he said, sweeping his right arm in front of him."

"It's so beautiful now. Inviting."

"And there's a lot you can't see, like a new pump and filter and a new heating system, in the pool and in the room."

"So, shall we try it out?" asked Colleen. "How about just twenty-five laps tonight?"

"Let's go!" Sean responded.

They did their laps and Colleen got out of the pool to sit on the edge, not realizing at first that Sean hadn't followed her. He was treading water in the deep end. "What are you doing?" she asked him.

He had a big grin on his face. "Ever made out in a pool?"

She chuckled. "No, have you?"

"No, wanna give it a try?"

She looked at the reception window behind her.

"Don't worry, no one's here but you and me," said Sean. "I made sure the cleaners would be out of here by 11 p.m., and I double checked."

"So, this was your plan all along."

"Of course!"

"Well, in that case . . . ." She started to slide into the pool.

"Nooo, no swimsuits." And he held his own suit out of the water and tossed it onto the deck.

"Can't I take it off in the water?"

"Nooo, I want to see you."

"You've seen me before!"

"Not from this distance. I want the whole picture this time."

"You do, do you? Well . . . ." She rose onto her

feet near the edge of the pool and began to slowly peel her swimmer's suit off her body, playing it like a striptease. And then she stood naked in front of him, made one complete turn. "Are you ready for me?"

"*More* than ready!"

She giggled and walked slowly and provocatively around to the ladder at the deep end and climbed down into the water, the better to keep him waiting. Then she submerged and swam under water to him. He submerged too and they grabbed each other's arms and pressed their lips together, fighting against their buoyancy to stay under the water for as long as they could.

And then suddenly Colleen jumped as her nightmare of weeks ago passed before her eyes. Rick, the beating, the blood. And she let go of Sean and broke away, forgetting to continue to hold her breath, and went to the surface coughing and sputtering.

Sean joined her. "Are you okay? What happened?"

She focused on getting her breath back and treading water for another few seconds, then replied: "I guess I forgot for a moment we were under water, and lost my breath."

"Are you sure you're okay?"

Colleen reached out and put her left hand on his face. "You're so sweet to worry," she said, but looking at his full, bare face suddenly gave her a stronger feeling of familiarity. She could now see the teenager in her yearbook, despite the lines on the older version. She remembered him now, the *real* him. It wasn't like recognizing his picture. She *knew* this face somehow. And then her hand touched something on the right side of his jaw, and she leaned over to see a jagged scar running along his jaw line. She gasped and pulled her hand back, and he turned and held her eyes in his.

"So what do you see in my Irish eyes *now?*" He asked. His voice had changed, lower and more guttural, and daggers had replaced the sparkle in his eyes.

"Sean?" And then she remembered, all of it. The ghost was fully formed and it was coming toward her.

She was sixteen years old, and she and Rick were at a house party. Rock music was blaring from a stereo system in one corner of the living room, which was full of other kids from school, some their friends, others she didn't know. People were yelling at each other over the music, many were drunk, and beer bottles were strewn everywhere, including the floor. The room was thick with cigarette smoke. Rick had gone to get his third beer, and she was standing with a few of her girlfriends, whose own boyfriends stood a couple of steps away, amusing themselves with each other.

And then a boy she recognized from some of her classes came up to her.

"Hi, Colleen," he said.

"She looked at the other girls, who turned to him and scowled.

"Hi," Colleen replied hesitantly. She didn't even know this guy's name. What was he doing coming up to her? He wasn't one of *them*.

He smiled at her. "I'm Sean Sullivan. I'm in your algebra and geometry classes."

She glanced at her girlfriends. They were whispering in each other's ears and pointing at him.

"I know," she said to him, taking a step backward. "What do you want?"

"I just wanted to tell you how pretty you look tonight."

Colleen stared at him. No one *does* that, she

thought. He was embarrassing her in front of her friends. "I just wanted to tell you how pretty you look tonight," one of the girls repeated back to him in a mocking voice. The others laughed like it was the funniest thing they'd ever heard. The corners of Colleen's mouth started to turn up. The voice *was* funny. She looked at the girl who had spoken; her eyes were crossed and she was bent over as if crippled. She looked back at the boy and saw the wounded look on his face, the smile on his face gone.

"Hey, what do you think you're doing, Irish?" said Rick as he arrived back with the beer.

Sean scowled at Rick. "My name is Sean,"

"I like 'Irish' better."

"It's not my *name.*"

"Well then, you shouldn't have told Coach you're Irish."

"The other boys joined in: "Yeah, Irish!"

"You still haven't answered my question, Irish," said Rick. "What were you doing with my girlfriend?"

"Nothing," Sean replied. "I was just talking."

"Well, go talk to somebody else!"

"Rick," said Colleen. "He's in my classes."

He turned to her. "I don't care. He knows

you're my girlfriend."

"You don't deserve her," said Sean, under his breath.

Rick "What did you say?"

Sean stood up to his full height. "I *said,* you don't deserve her."

And Rick's right arm shot out at Sean and hit him squarely on the left side of his face, throwing him off balance. He fell sideways over someone sitting at a glass coffee table, and hit the table, hard, and it shattered beneath him. He fell through it, slamming the right side of his face on the metal edge. When he managed to sit up, blood was pouring from a deep cut on the right side of his jaw line.

The kids sitting around the table edged away from it, and Rick stood over him. "You're Irish eyes aren't smiling *now* are they?" he said to him, and his friends gathered round him, laughing and patting him on the back, mimicking his punch to Sean's face. Then someone started singing: "When Irish eyes are smiling . . . ." and others joined in, though they didn't know any more of the words, only part of the melody.

In less than a minute, Rick and his friends turned away from Sean and joined Colleen and their girlfriends again. No one helped Sean up. Colleen saw him struggle to his feet, his right hand holding his jaw, and watched him make his way to the front door. He glanced back at her and she quickly turned away, back to her friends. She was not impressed with what Rick had done, but he was drunk, just showing off. They had already been dating a year and he was the best-looking boy in the school. Everyone thought they made a great couple and that they would be prom king and queen next year when they graduated. She didn't give the incident another thought.

Now, in the pool, Sean was watching her as the memory of that incident more than twenty-five years ago hit home. "Sean, I'm so sorry that happ—"

"You finally remembered," said Sean, his mouth tight. "I *knew* you didn't recognize me from high school, not really. I knew I'd have to shave off my beard before you would."

"You've been waiting for me to remember you? To remember what happened? Why didn't you just say something?"

"I wanted you to realize what you've been missing all these years. What you could have had if only you had given me a chance back then."

"I didn't *know* you back then, Sean."

"I tried to give you the opportunity to know me that night. I thought I saw something in you. I thought you might be different from the rest of them. But I was wrong."

"We were just kids, Sean. You know how high school is. You know I'm not that girl anymore."

"It's too late, Colleen." Sean paddled over to the ladder. "I'm leaving tomorrow."

"Leaving?" She paddled after him. "You mean all of this, these last weeks, was just to have me remember what happened to you? So you could make me feel bad about it?"

"Something like that," he said smugly.

"You're going to break up with me because of something that happened in *high school?*" She put her hand on his arm as he started to climb the ladder. "I thought you loved me."

He looked at her, a smile teasing the corners of his mouth. "You didn't know I was in the drama club, did you? No, that wouldn't be something you or your friends would be interested in. You just liked to party and get drunk and smoke pot."

She was stunned. "Are you telling me these last weeks were just an *act?* I don't believe it!"

"Believe it. I was actually a very *good* actor back then. I still do it on the side. Theatre is a bit of a passion of mine."

"Sean, don't leave, please. Let's talk about this. It's just a childhood grudge—"

He hissed at her: "Don't belittle it, Colleen."

"How can you leave? What about the club?"

"The owner arrives tomorrow."

"What? I thought *you* were the owner."

"Nope, I'm just the contractor he hired to get the house and the club renovated."

"The furniture, Diana's art?"

"Not mine, and never heard of her."

"*Everything* was a lie? We *talked, and* we made love . . . for *weeks!*"

"Yeah, it was fun. Thanks for the memory." He climbed out of the pool and walked to his swimsuit lying on the deck, pulled it on.

"Exactly how long have you been planning this?" she said to him as he walked by her on the way to the men's room.

He stopped and looked down at her at the bottom of the ladder. "You overestimate how much I cared. I put you out of my head right after your boyfriend bloodied my face, when you turned away from me at that party. But seeing you in this pool that first day brought it all back. An opportunity suddenly presented itself to make you feel how I had all those years ago. It was pure coincidence that I had a large reno to do in your neighbourhood. I live in Vancouver, but the owner knows my work and wanted me to do it. He told me I could use the house until he was ready to move in. He hired an interior designer to buy and place all new stuff in the house."

And then Sean turned his back to her and strode to the men's room, disappearing through the door.

Collen struggled to breathe, unable to move. She wondered if somehow she was back in bed, having another horrible dream, waiting to wake up. But it wasn't a dream. She was clinging to a ladder in a swimming pool, naked and shivering, chlorinated water from her hair running onto her face and stinging her eyes.

Family of Horses

The atrium of City Hall was quiet, but not empty, when Alicia arrived. The chairs lining the glass facade to her right held an assortment of people: a mother bundling up her toddler for the cold walk to the car; an early lunch-goer poring over a Harlequin novel while balancing a sandwich on her lap; a suited young man with a briefcase, looking at his watch, perhaps not wanting to be too early for an interview upstairs.

An elderly man in one of the chairs looked up from his newspaper as she stepped up from the north stairs onto the dark-blue patterned carpet. He nodded politely and went back to his reading. Most of the chairs were taken. She hadn't even considered that possibility, but there were two empties beyond the polite nodder, and she set her sights on the one two away from him, the last one in the row. She hurried to it, wondering what she'd have done if there hadn't been one, if her plan had been thwarted just when she'd finally found the courage.

Alicia set her briefcase on the floor, against the leg of the chair, and fumbled with the knotted belt of her coat. Warm with nervous energy, she removed the coat and folded it neatly over the back of the chair, then adjusted her sweater over her skirt and ran her fingers through the curls of her hair. She pulled the January issue of *Downtown* from her briefcase and sat. She glanced at her watch: only 11:30 a.m.

She opened her magazine and tried to concentrate on an article about the current live production at the theatre, but could see only the face of the man she couldn't get out of her mind, the one she was here to see. Blue-grey eyes framed by dark brows, aquiline nose surmounting a full moustache, square chin sporting a Kirk Douglas cleft. Her thoughts wandered to his deep, rich voice.

Behind her, warm air blew softly through large grated registers, keeping the cold windows crystal clear. She turned in her chair and looked out. Snow fell heavily, steadily, and she could just see the bronze stallion, blanketed in it, head held high and looking past his mate and her foal to "greener" pastures beyond. A snow blower roared up and down the front walk in a futile attempt to scrape away the constant, covering white.

She turned back to the atrium and watched the passers-by in the etched mirror on the interior wall: a man bundled up against the cold in a bright ski jacket—purple and red and yellow—tags swatting the nylon; a woman in a navy suit, hurried steps alternately echoing on salmon-coloured stone floor, then muffled as she crossed carpet rectangles set within it; a worker in beige coveralls, quietly polishing large silver planters, one by one, gradually making his way to the south end. She checked her watch again. Just fifteen minutes. She raised her magazine to her eyes. She still couldn't believe what she was about to do.

Among the murmurings of distant conversations and rustlings of her neighbour's paper, Alicia rehearsed the words she'd use when she saw him. If she saw him. She couldn't be sure it would happen today. She'd been several times already, but then lost her nerve before the lunch crowd even appeared. Today she was ready to go through with it.

"Hello again," he would say.

"Hello," she would reply, not too eagerly, in a voice that feigned surprise. If he asked her what she was doing there, she would say she was meeting a girlfriend for lunch and suggest they, too, meet for lunch, maybe next week. If instead he asked her to join him for lunch in the cafeteria, she would tell him she had an appointment and again suggest next week. She didn't want to eat with him here in City Hall; it didn't quite have what she was looking for. The lovely Sophia's restaurant was just across the street. Then he would know for sure she was interested in him.

She lowered her magazine and looked at the polite nodder seated just a few feet away. A tweed jacket peeked out from his heavy grey overcoat, which lay open and trailing to the floor. He wore a matching grey wool cap; white hair rolled in waves from beneath it and just reached over the collar of his coat. His profile sported wild bushy eyebrows, a prominent nose, a strong jawline. A good-looking man, probably in his seventies. She glanced at the thin gold band on his third finger. Years of marriage.

Alicia turned her left hand over and looked at her own band, dulled with scratches. Twenty years with the same man. Twenty years the same face, the same voice, the same life. A comfortable marriage. Predictable at least. But some days ill fitting. Two people working so hard to make themselves understood.

The atrium was noisier now. She glanced at

her watch. Five minutes to twelve. She opened her purse and looked for her mirror, checked her lipstick and hair, adjusted her silk scarf on her cashmere sweater. She ran her tongue over her lips.

The character of the passers-by was changing. Fewer ski jackets and boots, coloured mittens and scarves. Now dark overcoats and toe rubbers, white shirts with mostly conservative ties, and leather gloves. Groups of women in power suits and heels, walking quickly, chatting. Some carried lunch bags. As the offices spilled out their workers, Alicia's heart began to beat more furiously. She was beginning to feel a little obvious sitting here and a little too eager scanning the faces. A few of them glanced her way, but no one was familiar to her. And then, suddenly, the Hall was quiet again, only the occasional footfall in the distance.

Then she saw him, through the plants, beyond the information booth. He stood at the counter of the newsstand. She knew it was him, even though there was some distance between them. She knew his mane of salt-and-pepper hair and the grey suit, the same one he had worn that morning a few weeks ago at the tax workshop. She had arrived before him, but he had sat next to her. She had said hello, but he had started a conversation. She had said goodbye, but he had said see you sometime.

Alicia rose to her feet, gathering up her things, then saw that he had started in her direction, his coat over his arm, and sat back down, hurriedly rearranging herself. The old man looked at her and she smiled nervously at him. Then she turned back to the magazine on her lap, trying to calm her racing heart. She wouldn't look up. She'd let him surprise her.

An eternity passed.

Then she heard his voice.

"Dad," it said warmly.

She froze.

"Are you hungry?"

Her scalp tingled.

"Let's go. I've got a reservation at Sophia's."

She felt her face and neck redden. She didn't dare look, but out of the corner of her eye she saw the grey suit lean toward the chair, one hand extended. The older man rose and faced his son, faced her, drawing the younger man's attention to him, then took his arm and steered him back in the direction from which he had come.

Alicia turned her head to watch them go, and her eyes caught those of the father's looking over his shoulder at her. She continued to watch them after he turned away and placed a protective arm across his son's back, after they reached the south door and pulled their coat collars up around their necks, after they passed the family of horses and disappeared into the snow.

Legacy

Todd Chester squatted in the shadow of his Jeep, trying to get out of the blazing sun, re-reading the note his wife, Sarah, had left for him on the front seat under a small grey stone. The panic he had felt when he arrived at the abandoned vehicle and found her gone was dissipating.

He had expected her at the campground an hour ago. He allowed her a little leeway because she hadn't driven the Jeep much and was hauling his trailer behind it. He figured she was probably being overcautious and not driving as fast as he would. But an hour? It was too long. If she was in trouble she wouldn't be able to contact him; there was no cell service out here in the boonies. So, he borrowed his friend Gerry's truck and was at the Jeep in less than twenty minutes. "You were almost there, Babe," he muttered when he realized how close she had come to her destination.

Sarah's note was cryptic: "Jeep dead, need landline." And she'd drawn a little picture of a hill with a tree on it and an arrow pointing to it. The Jeep was definitely dead, and there was a little puddle on the asphalt beneath the oil pan. He'd picked out the tree she had headed to. It was off in the distance in the pasture across the road. He stood and looked again at the tree and then up and down the road. No traffic whatsoever. Other than walk to the campground, which would have taken hours, Sarah had done the only thing she could do: go find a phone. She had the landline number for the motocross track office, and they'd put any message for him there on the message board. He had checked it before leaving to find her, but there had been nothing posted yet.

Todd wasn't really worried. Sarah was nothing if not resourceful. She may have even found a landline since he left the track. He'd have to go back there to get her message, though.

He looked longingly at his trailer containing all his gear. If he wasn't alone, he could take it off the Jeep and hitch it to Gerry's truck, take it back with him now, but it was too heavy for him to move by himself, and it was parked precariously close to the ditch. If he tried and lost control of it, it would be disastrous. He couldn't risk it. Besides, he could get back to the track pretty quickly, get Sarah's message, and pick her up wherever she was. Gerry could help him tow both the Jeep and trailer back to the campground.

Todd double-checked that the Jeep's hitch and the trailer were locked and jumped back into Gerry's truck.

...

Sarah was tiring of the novelty of driving Todd's seventeen-year-old Jeep, especially with the hardtop off for the summer. The incongruous smell of baking bread and fresh manure coming from the wheat fields and pastures on both sides of the road assailed her nostrils as the air rushed over her; the road itself was full of potholes, adding considerably to the rough ride *normally* afforded by this vehicle; and after almost an hour of the engine roaring in her ears, she wondered if she would ever hear clearly again. "I guess you have to be a guy to like this," she muttered to herself.

She needed a break.

She watched for a field approach road, which she knew would usually be found every quarter section of land on the prairies, and she slowed her speed so she wouldn't miss the next one. Even though she had seen little traffic on this secondary road, it was uncomfortably narrow to stop on the shoulder. Todd was on one of his dirt bikes, somewhere between her and the campground at which she was to meet him. He had done some work on it and wanted to make sure everything felt right before the motocross tomorrow. She was pulling his other bike, and all the biking and camping gear, in the enclosed utility trailer. They had switched drivers about an hour ago, and Todd was going to take a maze of grid roads to the campground.

Sarah hated the thought of her husband on his dirt bike on *any* road that could have traffic on it, but grid roads held the additional danger of loose dirt and gravel. She hated him doing motocross even more. She hated the whole dirt bike thing, period. He'd already broken a leg once and cracked some ribs another time. He was getting too old for this nonsense. But there were two things he would not give up just yet: his Jeep and his dirt-biking. So, here she was driving his tin can of a vehicle, and going to a motocross she didn't want to attend, to watch her husband of twenty years risk life and limb. All because it was his birthday.

"Babe, please?" he had begged her earlier in the week. "Dale has bailed on me and I need to give the 450 a good run before I get there."

"Isn't Jeff going, too?" she asked.

"No, his bike's in pieces. The part he was waiting for still hasn't come."

"Todd, you know I hate those things."

"I know, I know. You're afraid I'll get hurt. But I guarantee nothing's going to happen to me."

She frowned at him. "You can't guarantee that!"

Now he was doing his puppy dog face: pouty chin to his chest and big brown eyes looking up at her. "Pretty please? I *need* you. And you don't have to watch if you don't want to."

"That doesn't make it any less scary for me."

"I'll be extra careful, I *promise*."

She looked at the white hairs that had recently emerged in his thick dark headful and wondered if he might soon quit anyway. He hadn't won a race in a while. The younger guys were leaving him behind. She sighed. "Okay, if you *promise*," she relented, knowing full well he'd always do the best he could against his competition, whether or not he was being careful. "I suppose I can't leave you alone on your birthday."

"Oh yeah, it'll be my birthday!" He grinned at her, showing the lines in his face, with which she was already very familiar, and then he gave her a big bear hug. "Thanks, Babe, I'll make it up to you."

"You don't have to do that," she said, but she pointed a teasing forefinger at him. "Just don't get hurt!"

Sarah now spotted an approach on her right and edged into it, watching the position of the trailer as she did so. Satisfied that she was off the road as far as she could be, she put the Jeep in park and turned the engine off. She climbed out and looked up and down the straight flat road. There was no traffic all the way to the horizon. She stretched her back and ankles, then reached into the vehicle for her water bottle and downed half its contents. She spread sunscreen liberally on her bare shoulders, which were turning pink, and after some more stretches and a few jumping jacks to revive her circulation, she was ready to go again. One last thing—a pee next to the right front tire—and she was back in the driver's seat. She checked the odometer before putting the vehicle in gear. According to Todd's directions, she had only twenty-five kilometres to go.

Sarah started forward slowly, turning the wheel slightly, then pushed harder on the gas pedal to pull away from the approach. She winced at the ugly screeching sound of the Jeep's undercarriage scraping hard across something, and then the vehicle stopped abruptly, throwing her against her seat belt. "Yikes," she said aloud. "What the heck did I . . . hit?"

She remembered before the question was complete. A boulder. She'd seen it on the far edge of the approach when she had pulled in and thought it must be there to prevent a person from inadvertently driving into the ditch. But she had been so focused on parking carefully, especially with the trailer attached, that it had gone out of her mind. She had walked in the direction of the trailer when she got out of the vehicle, to be sure it wasn't too close to the ditch, otherwise she might have been reminded of the boulder. She cursed herself as she put the Jeep in reverse and backed off, scraping the undercarriage again, her back teeth singing at the fingernails-on-a-blackboard sound.

Sarah prayed no significant damage had been done and got out of the vehicle to see what she could see, but everything was dark and dirty underneath, and she couldn't see a thing. She didn't really know what to look for anyway. She got back into the driver's seat and backed up as well as she could while nervously watching the trailer in the rear-view mirror, hoping she wouldn't dip its tail into the ditch. It appeared to be fine. Cleared of the boulder, she pulled once more onto the unforgiving road.

But she didn't get far. In less than ten kilometres the engine oil light went on. Her instinct was to pull over, but again there was the issue of the narrow road, and she'd left the flat prairies behind several kilometres ago. She had entered the gently rolling southwest corner of the province, and she didn't want to stop where oncoming traffic would not see her well. She really hoped the problem wasn't serious enough to keep her from getting to the campground. But then a horrible clatter started up under the hood, and she feared what could happen next. She hoped for another approach road, but even that was not to be. A sudden metal-on-metal bang caused her to jump in her seat, and the engine sputtered to its death. She used the momentum of the vehicle on a slight downhill to pull a little onto the shoulder, and then she came to a stop.

Sarah took a deep breath and let it out. Todd was not going to be happy about his Jeep, but the motocross didn't start until tomorrow, and that's all he would care about for the moment. He could probably get help from someone at the campground to haul his trailer there. It wasn't that far away now. He'd likely have to get a tow truck to haul his Jeep home, but he had insurance coverage for that. And she was sure he could get Dale or Jeff to pick them both up at the end of the weekend and take them and the trailer home. It was only a few hours away.

She grabbed her phone from her backpack and confirmed what she suspected would be true: there was no cell service on the highway. She saw no vehicles coming from either direction, but she couldn't see as clearly on the undulating land. All she knew for sure was she hadn't seen one in quite a while.

And it was *hot*. There wasn't a cloud in the sky, and the air was absolutely still; she could see it shimmering over the blacktop. Her phone told her it was almost noon, and neither the Jeep nor the trailer was casting much of a shadow. She would have no significant shade for a while, and she didn't relish sitting on the traffic side of the vehicle anyway, especially since Jeep and trailer occupied much of the right lane. And, unfortunately, Todd had the key to the trailer.

She had to get out of the heat.

On the west side of the highway was a wheat field, on the east a pasture. No cows in the latter as far as she could see, but in the distance she thought she saw a tree, perhaps more than one, standing out against the blue, cloudless sky. The top of a hill. She hoped it wasn't a mirage. Perhaps from that hill she could spot a farmhouse, which would likely have a landline she could use.

Sarah reached into her backpack for her small notepad and wrote a message to Todd, who would in time, she was sure, come looking for her. She grabbed two bottles of cold water from the small cooler in the back of the Jeep and put them in her backpack. She was glad she had thought to bring her red ball cap to take the glare off her sunglasses while travelling in the vehicle. She was seriously going to need it now. She took it off for a moment, removed the elastic from her ponytail, gathered up the stray hairs that had escaped, and put it again into a pony, which she pulled through the back of the cap. She slung her backpack over her shoulders and took one last look up and down the road. It was still empty. She crossed, plowed through the tall, dry grasses in the ditch, and carefully crawled through the barbed wire fence surrounding the pasture. She was on her way to that tree, and she hoped it offered a cool place to stop and a view of a farmyard.

...

There was no message at the motocross track when Todd returned, and he was starting to panic again as he rode in the truck with Gerry and his wife, Charlene, who were taking him back to the Jeep. It had been a couple of hours now and he feared Sarah could be lost or even hurt. His friends were going to haul the Jeep and trailer to the campground for him, get it off the highway before it caused an accident, and he was going to set out across the pasture to find Sarah. He was confident he *would* find her; she would leave "bread crumbs" in the form of notes for him along the way. It was her thing. He just hoped he found her safe and sound. He anxiously watched for the Jeep and trailer ahead, eager to get on her trail as soon as possible.

Todd and Gerry worked as quickly as they could to get a strong tow rope safely attached between their two vehicles. They had both sweated through their T-shirts by the time they were done. Todd grabbed a fresh one out of his duffel bag in the trailer, along with his ball cap, and both men splashed their faces with water from the cooler in the back of the Jeep. Todd noticed that Sarah had taken a couple of bottles with her, and he followed her lead and tossed a couple into his own backpack. At the same time, he grabbed the small emergency kit he kept under the driver's seat, hoping he wouldn't need it.

Charlene climbed behind the wheel in the Jeep, secured the seatbelt, and readied herself to guide the dead vehicle and trailer behind the truck. She had promised Todd she would check the message board at the track again when they got back, but Todd knew she wouldn't be able to reach him to convey any message. He told her he'd find Sarah, and a landline, and let her know where she or Gerry could pick them up.

Charlene waved to Todd as the caravan started off, and he waved back. Then he threw on his backpack, looked up and down the road, and crossed to the pasture.

...

After fifteen minutes, Sarah was beginning to regret her decision to walk to the tree. The clearly-long-absent cows had made a lumpy stew of the pasture, and her sandals gave her feet no support, especially on the hills, gentle as they were. There were also gopher holes to watch out for, collections of prickly thistle to walk around, and tall, dry grasses scratching her bare legs. Her ankles were now tight and sore, and she was sweating hard; a myriad of bugs were marooned on her sticky arms and legs. She stopped for a drink of water and looked back toward the highway, but she couldn't see it for the rising and falling of the land. She couldn't judge how far she'd come and whether or not to turn back. The tree she had spotted had gotten closer, however, so the lure of shade and a rest overcame her discomfort, and she continued on.

The crest of the hill delivered its promise. Sort of. It was a lone oak, large and highly branched, but it was entirely leafless. The tree was grey and brittle and very dead, she guessed from a lightning strike a long time ago. The huge trunk was split open part of the way to the ground. The tree was being held up by the intact lower few feet and undoubtedly by massive roots underground. That lower bit did cast a shadow to sit in, though, so she walked around the massive trunk to take advantage of it.

However, instead of a grassy space to sit in the precious shade, to her surprise Sarah found a tiny cemetery. The weathered grave markers closest to her were cracked open, the roots of the very tree meant to watch over them having split the markers as they emerged from the hill's surface looking for new ground. Tiny flowers, yellow faces drooping in the heat, grew from the cracks. Sarah knelt and ran her fingers down the wind-smoothed edge of the nearest marker and then over the surface, leaving finger trails in the layer of dust that covered it. She could feel the incised letters of the name of the deceased and wiped the surface clean, folding back withered blades of grass that corralled the marker. Her breath caught in her throat when she saw what it read. The smaller letters and numbers were illegible, but she could read the large block letters at the top of the dark grey stone: CHESTER.

Chester? She was a Chester; at least Todd was. She stared at the letters, then shrugged off her backpack and threw it aside. She set out on all fours, scrambling over the small area, pawing her way through the grass, looking for more markers. She wiped clean six of them arranged in two tight rows. The name was prominent at the top of each; they were all Chesters. Sarah sat back on her ankles, breathing hard, sweat running down her face. She stared at the graves, wondering about the lives of these Chesters, wondering if Todd was somehow related to them, wondering why she found them today.

After a few minutes, Sarah got to her feet and scanned the area below the cemetery. In the distance, to her right, she spotted clusters of poplar and fir trees. Vivid greenery, a veritable forest compared to what she had encountered so far, surrounded by sun-burnt hills. A valley? Where there was a valley and a stand of trees there was probably water. Her hot, sore feet screamed for it. In any case, it looked cooler there than here, the hills around it casting the trees in shadow. She couldn't see a farmhouse, but held more hope for one where more life apparently existed. She retrieved her backpack and wrote another note for Todd, took one last look at the grave markers, and then began walking down and across the hill, toward another promise of shade from the sun and potentially cool fresh water.

It didn't take Sarah long to reach the first cluster of poplars and, to her delight, a stream.

The slow-moving water was low, but it was probably the time of year. Lots of smooth rocks on either side told her it was often robust. She removed her sandals and stepped in, closing her eyes in the pleasure it gave her feet and ankles, then splashed water on her face, arms, and legs. She followed the water's flow toward the denser stand of trees, and the temperature dropped a few degrees as she hit the shadow, providing a cooling draft on her skin as she walked. A dozen steps into the trees and she noticed a dirt path alongside the stream. "Fantastic," she said aloud. "Where there is a path, there are people." She left the water and put her sandals back on.

It wasn't long before the stand of trees began to thin out again. And then, suddenly, a wide and seemingly flat valley opened in front of her. The stream and the path veered off to the left, following the edge of a stubble field dotted with golden-green hay bales that tickled her nose with sweet scent. On the other side of the stream was a wheat field, which appeared ready to be harvested. Ahead, at the far end of the two fields, was a hedgerow, a sure sign of civilization, though she could see nothing beyond it.

Sarah hurried along the path, which had now

turned into a track wide enough for a vehicle, and passed through the hedgerow. She stopped abruptly and gasped as she found herself in front of another cemetery to the right of the track. But this one was beautiful, light grey headstones standing in manicured green lawn, the whole of it enclosed in a white picket fence with sweet peas of all colours crawling over it. On the left of the track and across the stream was a field full of wild flowers. Another hedgerow ahead bordered both, and she could see that the dirt track continued through it.

This cemetery, surrounded on three sides by hedgerow, was large compared to the one she had found under the dead oak. She counted six rows of six headstones, with about three metres of space to the fence that corralled the neat-and-tidy square of graves. She began to feel uneasy, a stirring in her gut, as she walked slowly along the fence and past its entry gate. Every single headstone said "CHESTER" at the top, and she thought again of the tiny cemetery under the tree. So many Chesters. This must be a family farm that's been here for generations, she thought, and yet the headstones closest to her looked very new. She could read the black letters of the names in the first row—"Henry J.", "John S.", "Frank M."—but she couldn't read from this distance the smaller letters and numbers incised below them. As she approached the end of the row she noticed a newly dug grave, which sent a shiver up her spine, but before she got to it she heard her name being called from a distance. She looked toward the sound.

"Sarah?" A tall slim woman was coming through the second hedgerow toward her. She wore a long flowered summer dress, its hem brushing the heels of white sneakers. Her bare arms were darkly tanned, and her straight blond hair was swept up and held by an ornate hairpin. Sarah peered at her, wondering how she might know her, especially in the middle of nowhere. She waited as the woman approached, but even close up she didn't recognize her.

"Are you Sarah Chester?" the woman asked.

"Yes, I am," replied Sarah.

"I'm Beth. Beth Chester."

Another Chester. "Do I know you?" Sarah asked.

"No, you don't. But we were expecting you."

"Who was expecting me?"

"The family."

"The family? Whose family?"

"Todd's."

"Todd's? But Todd has no family."

"He didn't know about us, but we knew about him. Come and meet everyone." Beth turned and started walking back in the direction from which she had come.

Sarah paused for a moment. Todd has a family? He had told her he didn't. She wasn't sure she believed this woman, but she *had* said Todd didn't know about them. And then there were all the headstones with the name "Chester" on them. Her curiosity began to outweigh her hesitancy, and she decided to follow Beth. She needed a phone whether or not the woman was correct about Todd's relationship to them.

Sarah's jaw dropped when she walked through the hedgerow. There stood a beautiful two-storey house just beyond a huge vegetable garden planted on both sides of the dirt track. The house was the yellow of chick's down and trimmed in white, complete with dormer windows and a wide veranda. It angled slightly toward her, and when she passed the garden and got closer to the house, she saw that it overlooked a large, beautiful pond about five hundred metres away, complete with a surrounding marshland full of cattails and ducks. "It's so beautiful," she said.

Beth smiled at her. "It is, isn't it?" She led Sarah off the dirt track and onto green lawn, so she could get a better view. There was a bouquet of fragrances coming from flowers edging the house. Sarah breathed deeply and traced a variety of coloured blossoms along the yellow siding to the wide veranda to her right. Her eye caught sudden movement on the veranda; a strappy white sandal disappeared around the corner to the front of the house.

Sarah wondered how Todd could possibly be related to these Chesters and not know about it. He had told her his parents had died in a car accident when he was ten, and he had been cared for thereafter by an aunt on his mother's side. If the aunt had known of other Chesters, she hadn't told him, but apparently other Chesters had known of Todd. Why hadn't they contacted him?

Beth led her to the back of the house, where a Bernese mountain dog rose from the shaded porch and wagged its tail in greeting. "This is Sasha," she said, stopping and tousling the dog's big head.

The dog came to Sarah, who bent over her and

rubbed her ears. "Hi ya, Sasha." Sasha leaned in contentment against her leg, asking for more. While she rubbed, Sarah surveyed the area and saw a number of outbuildings set in the trees on the other side of the house, including a barn. In the distance was a pasture dotted with cows.

"We grow all our own food," said Beth, noting the direction of Sarah's gaze, "even the four-legged kind."

"When you say *we*?"

"The Chester women."

"The Chester *women*?"

"Let's go inside. You'll understand soon."

Beth was being very close-mouthed, Sarah thought. "I'll need to call Todd and tell him where I am," she said, "if you have a landline I can use."

"Of course," said Beth. "But that won't be necessary. He'll be here later."

"What?"

"Come in, Sarah. Everything will be explained to you."

Sarah's thoughts were racing. Todd was coming here? How did he know *she* would be here? *She* didn't even know where she was. Then her imagination put two and two together. The Jeep wasn't meant to break down before meeting him at the campground. Beth had contacted him and invited Todd and his wife to the house, and Todd wanted to surprise her. He was kind of a romantic that way. He'd pulled off many surprises for her before, and this would be a big deal for him, to find he had a family. Was there even a motocross going on this weekend? Come to think of it, thought Sarah, it was awfully coincidental that both Dale and Jeff couldn't go to it.

"I wasn't meant to arrive this way, was I, Beth?" Sarah asked.

Beth looked at her, gave her a little grin, but ignored the question. "Come in, come in. You have time to have a nice relaxing bath."

Beth clearly didn't want to ruin Todd's surprise completely, so Sarah didn't press her further. She stepped through the back doorway and onto a large mat overlaying the gleaming wood floor of a large, modern kitchen. She was suddenly aware of how filthy she was; a bath *would* be nice. She kicked off her sandals and put them outside in the porch, then closed the back door and followed Beth up a narrow staircase to the upper floor and through the second door on the right, one of many in a long hallway. The house was bigger than it had appeared outside.

"This is your room," said Beth as she stepped inside.

"*My*—"

"I hope you like it. You look out over the pond." Sarah followed her in and walked over to the dormer window and the little built-in bench it held. The view was magnificent. "You'll find a full bath just there," Beth went on, pointing to a door in the corner, "and something to change into in the wardrobe."

"But how—"

"When you're ready," said Beth, "come down the main staircase and turn right." She smiled at Sarah, her grey-blue eyes revealing nothing, but she suddenly seemed nervous, gripping her hands tightly together. She turned and left the room, pulling the door closed behind her.

Sarah surveyed the bedroom. It was a large space made cozy by rich dark furniture, including a queen-size sleigh bed with a plump duvet covered in olive green and ivory brocade. There were matching side tables complete with twin lamps, a dresser topped with fresh-cut wildflowers in a crystal vase, and a wardrobe. She opened the wardrobe to find a sundress and a pair of mules inside, probably loaners from Beth.

Clearly, they were expecting her, but she still wasn't sure how.

Sarah pulled her cell phone out of her backpack to find, again, there was no service, and to check the time. Todd would have expected her at the campground, if there even was a campground, a couple of hours ago now, so he had probably already found the Jeep. He would have to go back to the landline at the track office in order to update Beth, which was why she expected her. Unless there was no motocross. But if that was true, why would he give her a telephone number she could use to reach him?

The whole thing still didn't quite make sense. There had to have been an easier way to surprise her than hauling his bikes and all the camping gear to a non-existent motocross. And then he had left her to drive the Jeep while he test-drove his bike. That part of it made *absolutely* no sense. If it was a ruse, it was certainly an elaborate one.

Sarah's head was now spinning, her eyes were gritty with dust from the pasture, and she was exhausted. She wandered into the bathroom, where olive-and-ivory towels lay waiting for her. She looked into the bathroom mirror and then at the oversize bathtub, the bath salts, and all the toiletries provided, and she decided a thorough cleaning and a soak would work wonders, for her body and for her mind.

She luxuriated in the tub until her fingers and toes were pruney and emerged refreshed, but by the time she had dressed and had dried her hair, her mind was busy again. She'd been avoiding the "elephant" in the room, the thing that made even less sense than the motocross ruse: nobody could have predicted her Jeep breakdown on the highway. If she hadn't abandoned the Jeep when and where she did, she wouldn't have stumbled upon the Chester farm. Todd wouldn't have known where she'd end up, and Beth wouldn't have been expecting her.

She sat down on the bed and checked her phone again. She had been an hour in the bedroom. She hoped Todd was downstairs, ready to surprise her, but if he wasn't, the first thing she would insist on was using the landline. She'd call the number Todd had given her and confirm whether or not there was a motocross starting tomorrow.

...

Todd's second T-shirt was now soaked through, and the headband on his ball cap wasn't absorbing the sweat from his forehead anymore. He removed his cap and his sunglasses for the umpteenth time to wipe his face with the back of his hand. The sun was behind him but he could feel the back of his neck and arms burning. He wished he had changed into his shorts when he had the chance back at the trailer. The blue jeans he had worn on his bike were not making the hills any easier. But he had been anxious to find Sarah and hadn't thought of it. He wondered how she had managed to get through this pastureland, but he knew she would have. She had to get to the tree she drew in her note so she could leave her *next* note for him.

In the last few minutes, the thick grass he had been fighting his way through had started to whisper in a light wind that had come up. A glance over his shoulder had shown him a storm brewing in the northwest. He wasn't surprised. A hot day like this was bound to stir things up. The sun continued to shine where he was, though, and the tree was on the next hill, standing out against a cloudless blue sky in the southeast.

Todd didn't expect to find Sarah at the tree, but he hoped he could see something from there, something other than more rolling pasture. It seemed to be the highest point around. He wondered if this was the best direction for Sarah to head to find a farmhouse. Some of the farms in the province were huge; it could be hours before she found a home quarter, especially if she headed the wrong way. But whatever way she had chosen from the tree, he would have to follow, otherwise he would never find her. Suddenly a disturbing thought entered his mind: what if the people at the farmhouse she finally found weren't happy to see a stranger at their door? What if she stumbled upon criminals or, worse, crazies? "Nah," he muttered aloud. "That's just stupid!" But he glanced at the tree, within striking distance now, and pushed a little harder.

...

The main staircase was three doors away from the bedroom Beth had put Sarah in. A grand slightly curving affair of dark hardwood and wrought-iron spindles. She lightly traced the silk-smooth rail with her fingertips as she descended. She could hear voices below. She stepped off the last stair, then turned right and entered a large, beautiful room with richly upholstered furniture in baby blues and yellows. Natural light poured in from a bank of windows that offered an expansive view of the pond and the hills rising beyond it.

Seated upon two facing couches and several complementary chairs were Beth and five other women. They stopped their various conversations as Beth ushered Sarah into the room. Smiles greeted her as they rose and stepped toward her. One by one they welcomed her as Beth introduced them: Margaret, Maria, Gwen, Roseanne, and Andrea.

"Where's Lydia?" Beth asked.

"She's on the veranda," replied Maria. "She's having a hard time today." Sarah remembered the white sandal she had glimpsed earlier.

"You'll meet her later, then," Beth said to Sarah. "Let's sit down. I'll get iced tea for everyone." The women returned to their seats and Beth started to the kitchen.

"Is Todd still not here?" asked Sarah, holding her standing position.

Beth stopped and turned back to her. "No, not yet," she said.

"Then I'd like to use the telephone, please."

"Let's have a chat and something to drink first, Sarah," said Beth.

Sarah locked eyes with her. "Please tell me where the phone is, Beth."

Beth looked to Margaret, who appeared to be the oldest, and Margaret nodded to her. Beth led Sarah to another large room across the hall from the living room, which appeared to serve as both a study and library. An enormous antique desk sat in the middle, and the walls were virtually covered, floor to ceiling, with shelving packed with books. Several easy chairs with reading lamps were scattered around the room.

The telephone was on the desk. Beth left her alone to make her call, and Sarah unfolded the notepaper she had concealed in her left hand. She dialled the number Todd had given her for the motocross track office. The phone was answered on the second ring. The background noise of dirt bikes almost drowned out the voice of the man on the other end. Sarah had her answer: there *was* a motocross going on. But was Todd giving it up to come *here* for the weekend instead? She doubted it, knowing his obsession with the sport, but maybe he intended they have dinner here tonight and then set up at the campground.

The man on the other end was yelling "Hello" to her, repeatedly. She had to yell back. "This is Sarah Chester. I'm looking for my husband, Todd Chester. Has he been there today?"

"Say again? I can't hear a thing!"

She yelled her question again, this time louder.

"Wait a sec. I'll grab my registration list." He was only a few seconds. "Yeah, he's registered. I don't know him to see him, but I've got a checkmark next to his name."

"Can I leave a message for him?"

"Say again?" She said again, and he told her they had a message board and he would put the message on it. That's all he could do. She left the man her message: Sarah is at the Chester farm. She could think of nothing else to tell him. She had no specific directions for him because she didn't know where she was exactly, and she didn't know the return phone number to give him; Beth had disappeared. She wasn't too worried, though; presumably Todd had already spoken to Beth and knew where the farm was. The question of the day still nagged at her, though. How would he know she'd wind up here?

Sarah returned to the living room and sat in an empty chair next to Beth. A tall glass of iced tea had been placed on the table in front of it. She took a sip of it and surveyed the group in front of her. Margaret was perhaps in her eighties; Andrea appeared to be the youngest, perhaps in her mid-forties. If they were all Chesters, there was no family resemblance among them. They all seemed to be waiting in awkward silence for someone else to speak, some sipping their iced teas, some staring at their hands folded in their laps, all now avoiding looking at her. That uneasy feeling from the cemetery was stirring again in Sarah's gut. She tried to ignore it. So . . ." she started. "I can't believe I came across your beautiful home and that you're related to me, even if only by marriage."

Maria, sitting on the couch, looked across at Gwen, sitting in the chair opposite Sarah's. "We are *all* related only by marriage," said Gwen. "We are all wives of Chester men."

"Where are they, your husbands?" asked Sarah.

"You passed them on your way in," answered Margaret, looking at the gold band on her third finger, her years written in the blue veins showing through the paper-thin skin of her hands.

"I passed them? I didn't see anyone." And then Sarah realized what Margaret meant. "You mean in the cemetery."

Margaret nodded.

"All of your husbands are gone? How could this happen?" Sarah turned to Beth.

"Each of our husbands died in different ways and at different times," said Beth, "but the deaths were all accidental. Margaret's husband's car fell off a tire jack forty years ago. Andrea's husband drowned in the pond just five years ago. Mine had a fatal reaction to a bee sting twelve years ago." She paused, glancing at Margaret, who shook her head almost imperceptibly at her. "I'll spare the others."

"That's an amazing coincidence," said Sarah.

"It isn't a coincidence," piped up Roseanne, brushing unruly, curly brown hair off her face and reaching for her iced tea.

"There's more," said Beth. "They were all accidental deaths, but they all occurred when each man was on this property. And . . ." Beth paused, as if hesitant to go on.

"And what?" said Sarah.

Beth looked into her eyes. "Each man died on his fortieth birthday. We each arrived here on our husband's fortieth birthday, only to lose him on that day."

The Chester women seemed to be collectively holding their breaths, intent upon Sarah's reaction. She glanced from one to the next, her gut now clenched. Today was Todd's fortieth birthday. That's why she had agreed to go to the motocross. "What are you saying, Beth?" she said. "Todd planned a motocross weekend for us near a farm he wasn't aware of all his life, so that he could accidentally die on it on his birthday? That's crazy. He didn't even know you people existed until you called him!"

"I didn't say I called him, Sarah."

Sarah looked quizzically at her. "But you said he was going to arrive here later."

"Yes, that's how it works. We can't predict when and we don't know how he will die. We just know it will happen today."

"That's ridiculous! Even if I believed you, which I don't, we can call him and tell him not to come!"

"I'm sorry, Sarah, but we learned long ago that we can't stop it. The Chester men are drawn here by some unknown force."

Sarah scoffed. "Unknown force? You're kidding me, right? Did this 'unknown force' bring me here as well?"

"We think so," said Beth. Sarah stared at her, and felt her mouth fall open.

"Maria and I arrived with our husbands," said Gwen. "My husband and I got a flat tire on the highway, not far from the entrance here, and were looking for a phone." She looked at Maria. The two women looked a little alike, thin with sharp noses and glasses.

"And my husband and I were on our bicycles, headed to the provincial park," said Maria. "I slid on the gravel at the side of the road, fell into the ditch, and broke my wrist. My husband doubled me on his bike and brought me here. We could see the house in the distance."

"It doesn't matter," said a small voice coming from the hall. Sarah turned toward it.

"Sarah," said Beth, "this is Lydia. She arrived just two months ago."

Lydia stood barefoot at the entrance to the living room, in cropped jeans and T-shirt, white sandals hooked over two fingers. She was clearly younger than anyone else here, maybe in her early thirties. Her eyes were swollen and red from crying, but her chin-length dark hair framed an otherwise beautiful face. She hugged herself as if cold. "It doesn't matter how we got here," said Lydia, her voice shaking. "We're stuck in this nightmare together!"

"What do you mean?" said Sarah, looking back and forth from Lydia to Beth.

"Lydia," said Beth. "I was just explain—"

Lydia broke into sobs, turned, and ran up the stairs. Sarah listened to her footfall down the hall upstairs, and then a door opened and banged shut. Beth turned back to Sarah.

"I'm sorry, Sarah. Lydia is overwrought. We've all been through it. It isn't easy."

"It's the Chester *men* that are important, Sarah." It was Margaret, oldest and wisest, speaking now. "The unmarried ones arrive alone but, unfortunately, the married ones bring their wives along."

"But I arrived here alone and by accident. I didn't even know this was all here."

"You're not the only one that can say that," said Roseanne. "I arrived alone, too."

"But Todd is not one of your Chester men. He told me he had no family. His parents were killed in a car accident when he was ten."

"We know," said Margaret.

Sarah looked at her. "You know? Then . . . Todd's dad?" Sarah glanced at the window that overlooked the gardens.

"Yes, Todd's father, Matthew, and his mother,

Rita, are buried together in our cemetery."

Sarah's mouth was suddenly dry. "How?" she croaked.

"Their car went out of control on the hill during a winter storm. It flew over the ditch and landed on the property."

Sarah looked at the faces of the other women. Every one of them was looking at her now, a deep sadness in their eyes. Her hand shook as she reached for her glass of iced tea on the coffee table. She took a long drink. "How do you explain it?"

"We can't," said Margaret matter-of-factly. "It's always been this way."

"I've researched our particular Chester lineage thoroughly, Sarah," said Beth. That's why I was expecting you."

"There are other lineages?"

"Yes. They don't seem to be affected by this, whatever *this* is."

Sarah leaned forward onto her elbows, shaking her head. "So, we just happen to be the unlucky ones," she muttered.

"I guess you could say that, but we have a good life here together," said Beth. "A beautiful farm, everything we need and want."

"Why do you stay?" said Sarah, speaking to all the women collectively. "At close to forty years of age, all of you still had a lot of years left. You could have remarried, gotten on with your lives."

Lydia's voice came again from the hall: "Because we can't go."

Sarah sat up straight. "What did you say?"

"Lydia's right, Sarah," said Beth. "All of the wives of the Chester men of our lineage have lived here from the point of their husbands' deaths."

"What about your families, your children?"

"If there were children, they were grown up by then. Luckily, none of us had sons. As it happens, Todd is the last of our line, as you had no children."

"And you are, therefore, the last wife," added Roseanne.

"The people in our lives," continued Beth, "came to understand what we *told* them: it was our choice to move here. They can visit, but—"

"Choice? But Lydia said you were stuck here."

"We are," said Gwen. "We can walk for miles, but we always end up back at this house."

Sarah stared at Gwen, trying to process all the information she had been given, looking at each of the other women in turn. And then a smile began to form on her face and she slowly leaned back in her chair. "No, no, no," she said to no one in particular, and she started to chuckle. "I can't believe I almost fell for this. You just about had me, with the cemetery and the 'unknown force.' Who are you people? Did Todd put you up to this? This is by far the most elaborate—"

"Todd didn't put us up to this, Sarah," said Beth with a straight face.

Sarah laughed. "You're good, Beth. You're really good." And her eyes darted once more to the faces of the other Chester women.

They weren't laughing.

And suddenly the possibility that they might be telling the truth slipped into a corner of Sarah's consciousness, and the smile disappeared from her face. She jumped to her feet. "You're all insane!" she said. But it wasn't insanity she saw in their eyes; it was pity. She waited for someone to say something. No one did. And suddenly her skin was crawling and a high-pitched whining started up in her ears. "I'm leaving," she said firmly, looking past them and out the window to the beautiful pond. "I'm going back to the Jeep. Todd will be waiting for me."

"It won't work, Sarah," said Beth.

But Sarah ignored her. She headed to the hall and brushed past Lydia, who had come down from her bedroom and was sitting at the bottom of the stairs. "She's right, you know," she said to Sarah, her sad brown eyes welling with tears. "We all tried."

But Sarah refused to accept it. This had to be one of those very realistic nightmares she sometimes had. She would wake up if she could just get back to the Jeep. She fought to keep all other thoughts out of her head and hurried up to the bedroom, her heart pounding. She struggled back into her dirty clothes, grabbed her backpack, and left the house the way she had come in, passing no one in the hall or the kitchen.

No one tried to stop her. Somehow that scared her even more.

...

The wind had gathered force and the tall grasses were whipping mercilessly at Todd's blue jeans. The storm was advancing on him more quickly than he expected; the northwest was dark with angry black clouds. But the tree was within reach. He was on the final push up the hill to it. He could see now that it was dead, its scraggy, cracked limbs devoid of any small branches, the large ones swaying eerily in the wind. A few minutes later he was there, frantically looking for Sarah's note, praying the wind hadn't taken it away. There it was—a stone as big as his hand clearly out of place at the base of the grey trunk. He lifted it carefully and grabbed the note.

"Check out the grave markers," it said. Grave markers? He looked around and spotted something on the other side of the tree. Sure enough. Six of them. He removed his sunglasses to read the name at the top of the nearest stone. The wind caused his eyes to water and he shaded them with his hand and bent over to see it. "CHESTER?" he said aloud. He frowned. That was quite a coincidence. Sarah must have thought so, too. He checked out the other stones. All Chesters. But they couldn't be related to him; he had no family. "Must be a different Chester," he muttered.

Todd stood and looked at Sarah's note. She had drawn another arrow, this time pointing to two hills and a grove of trees between them. He spotted them below and to his right. The sun was suddenly obscured by the advancing storm, but he could see poplars down there, blowing frantically in the wind. Then he saw something else out of the corner of his eye. Something red was appearing over the swell of the hill. And then he recognized the ball cap; it was Sarah. His heart jumped to his throat. He had found her, and she was safe. He wasn't sure she could see him. He waved at her with both hands, trying to catch her attention, and called to her, but the wind snatched the words from his mouth. More of her appeared, he could see her waving at him, too, and shouting to him. He couldn't hear a thing.

...

Sarah picked up her speed as she passed the garden, and she glanced at the empty grave as she ran past the cemetery, the one that completed the square of graves. The headstone said "Todd W.," and she gasped. When she reached the path through the trees, the leaves of the poplars were rustling. She hit a wall of hot air on the other side, and a howling wind blew into her face hard enough to tear her breath away. She coughed and turned away for a moment to reclaim it. The wild grasses stung her legs as she started up the hill, looking for the dead oak. She leaned into the wind and the rise of the land and soon had to stop to catch her breath. She could see the oak now, standing out against dark cloud in the northwest, its heavy limbs beckoning her.

And then she saw a head and shoulders emerging from the top of the hill, and realized who it was. "Toooddd!" The wind tore his name from her mouth. She pushed forward, her feet leaden. A few more steps and she looked up again and there he was, standing at the top of the hill. He had spotted her, and his arms were above his head, waving at her. She screamed at him, "Go baaack," but she knew he couldn't hear her. She gestured frantically at him, but she knew he couldn't understand what she was trying to convey.

And then Sarah stopped. Her spine tingled as every hair on her body rose. She raised her head slowly. The sky had suddenly become an ominous black, as if a large paint can had spilled its contents on heaven's floor. It had moved over Todd, the oak, and the tiny cemetery. It splashed over the sun and the day plummeted into darkness. She looked up at Todd but could barely see him. He was waving frantically at her, urging her to join him. But she was rooted where she stood.

She knew what was going to happen.

The unbelievable was about to become

believable. Fleeting thoughts of what her future held for her played with the edges of her sanity, the faces of the seven women in the yellow house passing before her eyes.

And she watched in horror as a blinding jagged streak of lightning sought a greeting in Todd's outstretched hand and met its mark, striking him dead beneath the shattered tree guarding the Chester legacy.

Making It Real

Sondra stared at the blinking black cursor on the empty document page, fingers just touching the keyboard, waiting for the words to come. She glanced at the clock: 11:55 p.m. She was early, as always, but that was half the fun. She didn't know why the words started to flow at midnight, but she could feel the adrenalin kicking in, her heart beating a little faster, her cheeks flushing, as midnight approached. She was excited to see what this night would bring to the page but, at the same time was afraid it wouldn't bring a thing. How could this possibly keep up? How could the words flow so effortlessly, so enjoyably, night after night?

The night it started, Sondra lay awake in bed, mulling over her disastrous writing day. The story wasn't working; it was too predictable. She was doing everything right, everything she'd learned about writing a novel, but it felt forced. And so she tossed and turned, going over in her head what she had so far, renaming the heroine, changing the ending, hoping something would click. But nothing did. Her gut told her the story idea was fine; it was the telling of it that wasn't.

And then it came to her. She knew what was wrong. She was trying to write the story the way she was *supposed* to, instead of the way she *needed* to. She was trying to incorporate all that she had learned, instead of letting it flow naturally. And she was trying to mimic other authors' styles, instead of using her own.

Sondra got out of bed and threw her bathrobe on over her pajamas and thrust her feet into her slippers. She went to her office, closing the door quietly behind her. She switched on the light and put every writing how-to book cluttering her desk back on the shelves covering the wall opposite. Then she switched the light off again, the better to shut out the distraction of them. She sat in front of the glowing screen of her computer monitor, pulled up the folder containing the writing she had done thus far, and deleted all of it. She was too excited to sleep now, so she opened a new blank document and began. She glanced at the digital clock on the lower right corner of the monitor. It was midnight.

And her fingers flew for four hours. And then stopped.

She glanced at the lower left corner of the screen for the word count. She gasped; she had five thousand words, exactly. She sat, staring at the screen, unable to believe it, massaging her hands. She couldn't be sure if what she saw there was any good, but she didn't want to read it just yet. For tonight she wanted to hold on to the exhilaration she felt at reaching this point. And she sensed the writing was going to be just fine. At least it was a start. That's all she needed.

The next day Sondra read what she had written and was astounded at how good it was, considering it had felt more like stream of consciousness the night before, not writing like she usually did: slowly and meticulously. Other than fixing typos, she decided to leave it alone for now. She would have to do rewrites and editing later anyway. She might as well let the story play out. At the same time, she decided that if writing in the middle of the night always worked this well, maybe she shouldn't mess with it.

She didn't do any writing all day and went to bed with her husband, Brad, at their usual time and set her alarm for midnight. She was wide awake ten minutes before it was going to ring. She turned it off, so it wouldn't disturb Brad, and headed to her office, then went to the bottom of her previous night's writing. She couldn't write a word. Nothing came to her. She had no thoughts, no ideas. She re-read the last paragraph on the page, hoping it would stimulate her to continue. It didn't. She could feel the acid in her stomach bubbling up to her esophagus. "I can do this," she muttered out loud. "There's no way last night was a fluke." And she closed her eyes, took a deep breath, and tried to stay calm. And then a tingling sensation started in her fingers and her hands suddenly warmed. She glanced at the clock. It was midnight.

She started typing.

And four hours later she had another five thousand words, exactly. And she massaged her hands, put lubricating drops into her dry eyes, and went back to bed, trying not to think about the crazy numbers. After the fourth night, she stopped setting her alarm—she always woke at ten minutes to midnight—and she stopped expecting to write *before* midnight—it always started exactly then. It was a little disconcerting. It occurred to her that she'd somehow wandered into Rod Serling's *Twilight Zone*, but she was writing her first novel, finally, and she tried not to think about *how*. She only hoped it would last.

And now, here she was again at 4:00 a.m., for

the seventh time, done for the night. She looked toward the window a few feet to her right. At first she saw only her own reflection in the glass, the computer screen the only source of light in the room. Then she saw that it was snowing. Large flakes swirled madly before catching and settling on the sill. She rose and arched her back, stretched her arms to the ceiling, and put her two sore hands on the cold glass.

...

Sondra sat at a table by the window in The Coffee House, glancing at the clock, then out to the parking lot, back and forth, unable to remain still while she waited for her friend Carly to arrive. The place was buzzing with conversation, every table taken, every chair draped with winter parkas, sleeves stuffed with wet scarves, toques, and mittens. The nails of her forefingers tapped against the large mug she circled with both hands. She had finished her coffee already. She headed to the counter with her empty cup and ordered another, placing a handful of change in the palm of a young man with shocking red hair, who stood behind the counter.

"You started without me?"

Sondra jumped at the voice suddenly behind

her. Carly stood inside the door, unwrapping a large red scarf from around her head and neck, releasing a mass of dark curls down to her shoulders. Her nose was pink from the cold, and her tortoise-shell glasses were completely fogged over in the heat of the shop.

"I was here early," said Sondra, "so I'm on my second cup." The redhead placed Sondra's black coffee on the counter and waited for Carly's order. Carly grabbed a napkin off the counter to wipe her glasses and then, vision restored, gave the young man her latte order and removed her bulky parka. Sondra led the way back to the table, where they sat opposite each other.

"Well, what's up?" said Carly as she settled in. "I walked the whole way here and it's freezing outside. I can't feel my toes! So, give it up."

"I've been writing," said Sondra. "A lot."

"Of course you have. You're a writer."

"Not like this. I've had five thousand words every day for the last thirty."

"Wow, you're on a roll!"

"It's more than a roll. I've written a novel in a month. One last chapter tonight and I'll be done."

"It's not unheard of."

"This is *me* we're talking about, Carl. It's

unheard of for *me*."

A shout-out from the redhead and Carly jumped up to fetch her latte. When she sat down again she warmed her hands on the mug before taking a drink. "So, your muse finally arrived."

"Well, something has. I don't think it's my muse."

"What do you mean?" Carly put her lips to her cup.

"I don't think it's me writing, exactly."

Carly lowered her cup to chin level, rested her elbows on the table, and looked at her. "What?"

"My fingers are on the keyboard, my butt is in the chair, but I don't write a word until midnight, and then it starts on its own. I mean, my fingers start typing and I can't stop them. I don't want to stop them—I mean, the writing is good—but then four hours later, *exactly*, it stops on its own. I mean, my fingers stop typing. And I can't start them again, even if I want to."

Carly stared at her, her cup still held in front of her chin. "You're kidding me, right?"

"No, I'm not." Sondra lifted her own cup, reluctant to look her friend in the eyes, and drank.

Carly put her cup down on the table, studied

it a while. "Look, you've gotten yourself into a routine, that's all. And if you're writing during the night, you're probably not getting enough sleep."

"I sleep until noon every day. That's a full eight hours. I don't even hear Brad get up and go to work."

"Well, then, your routine is simply working for you. You get into the zone and it comes so easily you can't believe you're writing it. Isn't that what you've always wanted?"

"Yes."

"Then what's the problem?"

Sondra looked down at her cup of coffee, unsure of how much she should tell her friend. She was already sounding crazy. Carly was right—she had simply gotten what she wanted. She was writing like she'd never written before, and she was about to finish her first novel. But there was something unnatural about it. It was more than her eerily exact word count; she felt like the story was out of her control. And it was scaring her.

Sondra looked into Carly's brown eyes. "The problem is I don't know how the story's going to end."

"Isn't that a good thing?" asked Carly. "Didn't you tell me once that a story essentially writes itself? You can't force it one way or the other?"

"Yes, but you're in it this time, and things aren't looking so good for you."

Carly sat back in her chair and smirked. "I'll try not to take that personally," she said, "but it's *horror* isn't it? Things usually aren't good for *someone* in horror fiction."

"Yes, in fiction." Sondra paused. "But what I've been writing has become horribly *real*."

Carly stared at her. "What does that *mean*, Sondra?" Her brows furrowed and she folded her arms on her belly, annoyed.

"Last night I wrote the scene in The Coffee House." She looked around the room. "And here we are."

Carly leaned over the table and looked at her over her glasses. "You invited me for coffee this *morning*."

"I wrote that part too."

Carly sat back up in her chair, staring at Sondra, her mouth tight. She sipped her latte. Seconds passed before she spoke: "What the hell are you telling me?"

Sondra held her friend's eyes in hers. "Something's going to happen to you, Carl. Something bad."

"And I suppose you wrote that, too."

Sondra nodded and looked down at her cup. "Remember that apartment fire last week?" she said quietly.

"What?"

"Chapter Seventeen."

Carly looked around the coffee shop as if afraid other people might hear what her friend was saying. She hissed at her. "Listen to what you're saying, Sondra. You think you're writing the future? You sound like a lunatic."

"It's not *me* writing, Carl. I swear."

"Uh huh. And just who do you think it is?"

"I dunno, some . . . *being*."

Carly put her cup down and rubbed her temples with her thumbs. "Some *being*?" she said under her breath. "Really?" She got up, grabbed her coat, struggled into it. "I gotta go."

"Don't go, Carl, please. Come back to my house with me. Stay over. See the story for yourself."

Carly turned and walked to the door.

Sondra watched her friend wrap her scarf around her neck and face, pull the hood of her parka up, and step out into the cold. She held her breath as Carly headed across the parking lot and disappeared behind a hedge. She waited for it, And then it came: the crash of one car into another and the thump of the latter into human flesh, the two vehicles unable to stop on the slippery street, unable to keep from rolling over Carly's body, despite slamming on their brakes. The cracking of skull bones and the squishing of the soft tissue within as a tire came to rest directly on her head.

Exactly as she had written it.

...

"Are you there?"

Of course.

"I'm going to finish it tonight, aren't I?"

Yes.

"I'm not sure I want to."

Why not?

"I don't want to hurt anyone else."

You have to let the story take you where it needs to go.

"The story? I don't even *know* the story until I read it the next day!"

That is not true. You have been writing it.

"Me? You're the one—"

It has always been you.

"No."

Yes.

"But I'm hurting people."

Yes, it is a horror story.

"I mean in real life."

You are not hurting people in real life.

"But I thought—"

You are making the story feel *real, yes."*

"People aren't really dying?"

Of course not.

"But I saw online . . . the fire."

You haven't been on the Internet in thirty-one days.

"I don't understand."

You have been living and breathing the novel, Sondra.

"I have? But it was so real."

As I said.

"So, Carly's ok?"

The character?

"No, the real Carly. We met for coffee—"

You have not left the house in thirty-one days.

"I haven't?"

As I said.

"Who *are* you?"

Writers like to call me their muse.

"What are you *really*?"

Your resolve, no more.

"My resolve?"

Yes. Now, are you ready to begin?

"Yes."

Good. Then carry on.

Sondra glanced at the clock.

It was midnight.

Coffee and Tea

Carol didn't know he lay dead beside her.

She was dragged from a dream involving family, in the dining room of her childhood home, into her ice-cold bedroom when the dog's wet nose found her arm sticking out of the bedcovers. She drew the frozen limb back beneath the heavy warm layers. "Saaaleee," she moaned, blinking hard, trying to bring herself into this familiar place, pulling away from steaming Christmas turkey and the din of spirited conversation to crisp, still air. Her eyes found the horizontal blinds on the window, the narrow doorway of the ensuite bathroom, the straight edges of the dresser. She rolled onto her right side and peered at the red numbers of the clock on her bedside table: 6 a.m. Way too early for a Saturday. Way too early for a Saturday in January. But Sally didn't know it wasn't a work day.

"Jack," she muttered to the mound beside her, "Sally needs to go out." He didn't stir, but that was a favourite trick of his. He knew she wouldn't make the dog wait. She pushed herself up to a sitting position and groped with her feet for her sheepskin slippers. She climbed quickly into her terrycloth robe, trying to capture the warmth from her pajamas, then felt her way to the dark hall on Jack's side of the room. She partially closed the door behind her, so the light wouldn't disturb the heap in bed.

Sally led the way down the carpeted stairs to the back door, her nails clicking on the checkerboard floor in the kitchen a reminder the golden retriever needed a grooming. Carol flicked the outdoor light on and opened the door, and frigid air rushed in. Sally raced out to the lawn, leaving tracks in the fresh snow on the concrete patio. The lawn was now buried by at least a foot of the stuff, and it was still snowing. She headed to the coffeemaker.

Before Carol could press the switch to ON, Sally was back, and her four snowy feet slid a little as she rushed across the floor, eager to return to the coziness of her dog bed. The dog knew the routine: ten minutes while the house warmed up, then breakfast. Carol followed the furry six-year-old back to the bedroom, adjusting the thermostat on the way.

Back in bed Carol pulled the covers over her nose and waited for the warmth beneath the blankets to wrap itself around her once again. She heard the furnace kick in and relaxed in its comforting hum, turning onto her left side, as was her habit, to the mass that was Jack. "Coffee's on," she said as she touched his bare, cold shoulder. That the man slept in the buff in the middle of winter still amazed her, and she pulled the covers up to his chin. "Jack, you're freezing." He didn't respond. She nudged him. "Are you awake?" Nothing. "Jack?" Even on a Saturday, his workday routine would wake him by now. There'd be a grunt, a movement, something. Her stomach lurched. "Jack, wake up!" Still no response.

Carol whirled around and out of bed and scrambled for the light switch at the door, hitting it with the heel of her hand, blinding herself with the illumination. She tripped over Sally, who had jumped into the action, and just managed to grab the headboard in time to keep herself from landing on top of her husband. She flung the covers back from his hairy chest and placed her right ear to it. She heard only the pounding of her own heart. She pressed her fingers against his neck. She felt nothing. She looked at his face. His skin was colourless against the maroon pillowcase.

She straightened to a stand at the bedside. She'd never seen a dead person before. Jack looked like he was still sleeping, but his mouth had fallen open. He never slept with his mouth open. She knew because she was awake often during the night. If the moon was full, shining into the bedroom, she'd see his eyeballs moving under the lids and wonder what he was dreaming. He was flat on his back now, eyes closed and quiet, both arms neatly at his sides, the position in which he started out every night and awakened every morning. She always told him he slept like the dead. Somehow she was not envious anymore.

Carol absently stroked Sally's head and looked at the man she lay next to for thirty-two years. Suddenly he seemed unfamiliar. Without the man she knew inside, it was just a body. How long did she lay beside it after Jack was gone? She shivered and drew the covers back up to his neck. She slipped her robe and slippers back on, picked up the telephone receiver sitting on Jack's bedside table, and pressed 911. "My husband appears to have died in his sleep," she told the man on the other end. He was sending a police unit and an ambulance, just to be sure.

She started down the stairs. She could smell the coffee now, dark and strong, the way Jack liked it. Suddenly her knees gave way and she sat down hard on a step. Her hands were shaking and pinpoints were popping in her vision. She struggled to keep from blacking out. The stairwell was suddenly too small, the house too big. For an instant she couldn't remember it. She tried to focus on the living room below, the weak light meted out by a front street standard falling on the couch on the far wall and the oversize matching chair perpendicular to it. And then she remembered her grandmother's maple nesting tables on the left and the large vase from her mother, with its tiny painted vines and pink flowers, on the floor on the right. The squeal in her head subsided.

Sally tugged at the cuff of Carol's robe, reminding her about breakfast. A few seconds with her face buried in the dog's thick fur, and then they headed to the kitchen. After filling the dog bowl, she filled her favourite coffee cup—the big one with Sally's picture on it—and took a chair at the kitchen table.

Now it was just the two of them: she and Sally. Carol hadn't dared imagine this moment. She was scared she might be devastated if Jack died, which would mean she was wrong; she *did* love him, they *were* right for each other, she *couldn't* live without him. But she was not devastated. Suddenly she could think of only one thing: she was free.

A hard knock on the front door made her jump. Sally growled low in her throat and led the way out of the kitchen. Carol looked through the peephole at the front door. "It's okay, Sal," she said, and the dog backed off and waited. Carol opened the door to a man in a police uniform and suddenly wished she'd gotten dressed. But then she remembered Jack's body lying in the bedroom and knew that, even if she had thought of it, she wouldn't have wanted to go back in there. A thought came to her from nowhere: what if she had made a mistake? What if Jack was not actually dead? Maybe she should have double checked before the police arrived.

The officer stepped in, followed by two paramedics. Carol realized she'd heard no sirens heralding their arrival. She was glad they decided there was no emergency. It was still dark outside and people were sleeping. The men kicked off their boots, and she directed them to the bedroom, then refreshed her coffee and sat at the kitchen table once more, Sally's head under her hand. She was holding her breath a little, nervous at what the men might find upstairs. She'd been on her own less than a half hour, but she already liked it.

"I'm sorry for your loss," the officer said to her when he came down to the kitchen some minutes later. She thanked him and answered his questions about Jack and the events of the morning. "The medical examiner is on his way," he said after he'd finished scribbling. "He'll need to officially verify the death and do a preliminary exam."

"Of course."

"I see no evidence of foul play."

"Foul play?" Something in Carol's stomach fluttered. "I didn't hear anything during the night." She wouldn't have, of course. She took something occasionally to help her sleep, and last night was one of those occasions.

"We have to be sure, that's all. The medical examiner will look for any signs on the body that might tell him cause of death, before giving us the okay to remove it. He will also do an autopsy back at the morgue."

"Of course."

"Was there anything unusual about your husband's behaviour the last few days? Any signs of stress?"

Carol assumed the officer must be thinking it was a heart attack that took Jack. "No, I didn't notice anything that had me worried."

"Nothing going on at work?"

"No, nothing I know of. He's busier now, getting ready for tax season, but he's been an accountant for twenty-five years. There's nothing new this year."

Carol was suddenly distracted by a man coming into her kitchen who looked like he just got out of bed. The white hair he had left was sticking out in all directions. He shed his parka and threw it over the back of a chair. It was the medical examiner. He nodded politely at her. The officer excused himself to accompany him upstairs.

She stood at the kitchen counter. She knew she should be more upset about Jack. The men upstairs might wonder why she was not. In time, maybe she would be. Maybe the enormity of her loss just hadn't set in yet. After all, she was used to having Jack around. He was company.

The two men returned to the kitchen within minutes. "I'll take care of this as quickly as I can," the medical examiner said to her in a kind voice.

"Thank you, I appreciate that," she replied.

"There's nothing external that points to a specific cause of death. I'll know more after the autopsy. If you could give the officer a list of any medications your husband was taking, that would be helpful."

"He wasn't taking any. Nothing I know of, that is." Another thought: could Jack have found her sleeping pills? She quickly dismissed the idea. It wasn't possible.

The medical examiner looked at her. "You think your husband might have been taking something you *didn't* know of?"

"No . . . I mean . . . I don't think so." She could feel her neck flush.

"Would you mind if the officer has a look around, maybe in your medicine cabinets, your husband's belongings, just to be sure?"

"Sure. That's fine."

"Thank you. He should check his office, too. And if there's anything further that comes to you that could be relevant, please contact the officer and he'll let me know." The medical examiner grabbed his parka and struggled into it as he left the kitchen. She could hear him grunting at the front door as he pulled on his boots, and then he left the house.

While the officer was back upstairs the paramedics walk past the kitchen with a gurney, Jack's body in a bag on top. Carol wasn't sure if she should ask for one last look, maybe say goodbye, but she hesitated too long and heard the front door opening and closing before she could decide.

The officer returned to the kitchen, rifled through drawers and looked in cupboards. He scanned his notes. "I have confirmed there are no prescription medications in the house with your husband's name on them. If you would give me the address of your husband's office and his office keys, and the name and number of his doctor, that should be all I need for now."

"Sure." Carol grabbed her address book next to the kitchen telephone and left the officer to copy down what he needed while she fetched Jack's keys from the hall table.

The officer handed her a card with his own contact information on it, and then she followed him to the front door and watched him walk away. It was still dark, but the snow had stopped falling and the streetlight cast his shadow across the yard as he headed to his car. Some lights were now on at the neighbour's house across the street. She sighed as she closed the door. She wasn't looking forward to the outpouring of sympathy.

Carol ascended the stairs to the bedroom, followed by Sally, who flopped into the dog bed for her usual after-breakfast snooze. Carol looked at the concavity in Jack's pillow, where his head was just minutes ago, where it would never be again. It was hard to believe she had the bed to herself after so many years of sharing it. Even when Jack was away on business she slept on her own side. She wanted to climb in right now, spread out, luxuriate in the freedom to turn over without constraint, but she was a little unnerved by a dead body having been in those sheets. She got out of her robe and pajamas and into old jeans and a sweatshirt. In two trips she took pajamas, bed coverings, and pillows down two flights of stairs to the laundry room in the basement. She started the washer on the first load and returned to the main floor.

As she passed through the kitchen on the way to the garage, Carol grabbed another cup of coffee. This was more than she usually drank in a morning, but it turned out she had made too much and she hated to waste it. She walked past the back door and opened another into her warm studio, leaving the door open for Sally. She congratulated herself, as she had every morning for the last five years, for finally insisting on the garage for herself and her painting. Jack had grumbled about his car having to sit on the driveway, but he couldn't argue when she offered to pay for the renovations herself. The surprised look on his face had definitely been worth the price. He had no idea how well her work was received. She glanced around at the new paintings hanging on the walls, then the piece she was currently working on, propped on the easel. The rich reds and yellows in these recent canvases pleased her, and she smiled.

The grey light coming through the skylights in the ceiling told her the sun was finally on the rise. It was no good for painting yet, but she had a new idea and headed to her drafting table, where she ripped a large sheet of newsprint off the roll attached to the wall above. She sat on her stool, turned on the lamp reaching over the table, and chose a flat, soft pencil among many sitting in an old Mason jar in which her grandmother had once preserved peaches. A small teapot standing next to the jar caught her attention and she laid the pencil down.

The teapot was dog-shaped. It was Sally, according to the five-year old niece who gave it to her years ago, though it looked nothing like a golden retriever. The right paw was raised to form the spout, and the tail was the handle, broken long ago and held together with glue. She picked up the pot and lifted the lid. She used the pot for her erasers...and one other thing.

Carol shook the contents of the pot until she saw it, then squeezed her fingers inside, grabbed the small prescription bottle, and returned the pot to the shelf. She popped the top off the bottle and carefully dumped the contents onto her paper. Twenty-two pills. Just as there were last night after she took the one she wanted. She kept a careful count, mostly to be mindful of her own use. She was not really worried that Jack had found her pills. He didn't know she was taking them and he hadn't stepped foot in the garage since the renovations began. He didn't care about her art any more than she cared about his accounting.

She sighed as she returned the pill bottle to the teapot. An artist and an accountant. Could two people be more different? How they looked at things, what they liked to spend their time doing, where they expected to be at the end of it all? She thought not. But it was true what they said—love is blind—and she was young when she fell in love with Jack. Nobody told her that at eighteen she couldn't possibly know who she was and what she wanted out of life. She probably wouldn't have believed it anyway. And by the time she had given up struggling to fit with someone who didn't fit her, twenty years had passed. While she came to grips with it, another seven. Then she changed gears and threw her passion into her art.

And she told herself it didn't matter anymore. If she had her painting, she could settle for companionship instead of love, routine instead of spontaneity, satisfaction instead of fulfillment. She reached a level of comfort, finally, with Jack, and she decided what she knew with him was better than what she didn't know without. Still, she wished. She wished for a life of her own making. One without schedules and budgets and order. One with affection, discovery, and joy.

One without Jack.

An image suddenly jumped to mind of the rumpled medical examiner bent over Jack's body lying on a stainless steel table. No, he wouldn't find drugs in Jack's system, but when he opened him up he might not even test him for drugs.

Because he'd find something else.

"It's an aortic aneurism," the nurse had reluctantly told Carol on the phone yesterday when she couldn't reach Jack at his office. It was nearly 7 p.m. and the end of her shift, and she wanted to talk to him before she left. But she also didn't want to be responsible if something happened before she could. "It's a swelling of the wall of the main artery transporting blood from the heart to the rest of the body," she explained, "and he needs to be scheduled for surgery right away to repair it."

"It's *that* serious?" asked Carol.

"It's *very* serious. It could rupture with no warning and it could kill him."

"But I'm not expecting him home until very late tonight. He's with clients."

"Does he have a cell phone with him?"

"Yes, but he always turns it off when he's with clients."

There was a pause at the other end of the phone. The nurse was clearly conflicted. "Well," she said finally, "the admissions desk is open 24-7. Get him to call as soon as he *does* get home."

"I'll tell him to call as soon as I can," Carol promised. But she knew within seconds of hanging up the phone that she wasn't going to tell Jack that night about the call. He was schmoozing: wining and dining and talking business. He didn't expect to be home before midnight. She could leave a message on his cell phone to call her but there was no point. He'd be on his way home when he listened to it and would see no *need* to call her. She could leave him a note on the hall table, but he wouldn't thank her for it. He'd arrive home tired and wound up, and he'd be in no mood to deal with the hospital.

So, when 11 p.m. arrived, her usual bedtime, Carol took her sleeping pill and headed upstairs with Sally. She was pretty sure something that had taken some time to develop, as the nurse had told her the aneurism had, was likely to take Jack through one more night. Odds had always been in Jack's favour. She got into her pajamas, washed her face and brushed her teeth, and climbed into bed.

Within minutes of touching her head to the pillow, she heard the front door open and close.

Even Sally didn't budge.

Sally now wandered into her studio and headed to the door to the back yard, scratched on it as she always did. It was time for serious business. "Need to go out, Sal?" Carol asked. Part of the ritual. Sally wagged her tail and twirled in confirmation. With coffee mug in hand she went to the door and let the dog out. The sky had cleared and the sun was up, and she watched Sally snuffling the fresh, sparkling snow as she paced the yard, taking her time to find the best spot, despite the cold. Carol grasped her mug with both hands and drank. The coffee was dark and strong, the way Jack liked it.

She decided she'd make tea tomorrow.

The Doctor's Wife

Carrie lay on her back, then her right side, then her belly, then her left side, listening to her husband snore. It was like eavesdropping on a conversation but only hearing half of it. Quiet, then rattling on, sometimes polite: "I understand what you're saying"; other times insistent: "But *surely* you see the difference"; occasionally surprised: "You're kidding!"

She smiled to herself in the dark. Her writer's mind said, "You should write this down," but her Itty Bitty Book Light needed a new battery, and if she turned on her bedside lamp, her husband would wake and know she wasn't sleeping. Maybe guess why.

She started a story once—"I could have married a doctor . . ."—but couldn't finish it because she didn't know how it would end. She knew now, but she didn't *want* to finish it. She had lived too long with the fantasy.

Her husband rolled over, his back to her, and she adjusted her weight, rebalancing.

...

Carrie had arrived early to the press conference that morning, hoping to get a good seat, but she didn't know that the room designated for the event at the university was a lecture theatre, and that the university community would be invited. The theatre was filled to the doors, not one seat available. Dr. David Sanderson was considered the best heart surgeon in the country, and he was now, after twenty-five years, joining the staff at University Hospital, the teaching and research hospital where he'd earned his medical degree, in the city in which he grew up. The city in which *she* grew up.

On stage with the guest of honour sat the city's mayor and the health region's president and CEO, nodding to each other in congratulations, grinning like cats into cream. Dr. Sanderson would attract not only other noteworthy staff but patients to the hospital. Students would want to train with him, and money would flow to the university. He would put their city on the map. The first row of audience seats held suited hospital administrators and city higher-ups. She recognized a few of the faces from interviews she'd done over the years. The row behind the administrators was occupied by the doctor's new colleagues, most in white coats; the resident heart surgeons among them were there to size up the competition. In the rest of the seats were students, their laptops giving them away, and the walls were lined with reporters and cameramen.

From her position at the back of the theatre, Carrie couldn't distinguish David's features, but the set of his body, tall and straight, and the slight tilt of his head to the left was very familiar. And when he spoke, the rhythm of his words sent a shiver up her spine. She was suddenly back more than thirty years, sitting with him in his car in the parking lot overlooking the river weir, holding hands and talking, the late-summer moon shimmering on the water and the crickets chirruping in the tall, dry grasses.

She had arranged through the hospital to do a feature on David for *The Star*, but he wouldn't know her married name when he saw it on his agenda. And in this crowd of people in the theatre he wouldn't see her. Would he recognize her if he did?

When the questions to David and the two men standing with him waned after three-quarters of an hour, and students began to leave for their classes, Carrie left the theatre and made her way to the narrow hallway that descended to the lecturers' entrance. She stood away from the door and could feel the butterflies gathering in her stomach as she waited. How would he react when he saw her?

By the time David came through the door fifteen minutes later, a few reporters had joined her, ready to capture whatever further tidbits he might be willing to give them. He was accompanied by his hosts from the stage, but despite their protestations on his behalf, he stopped for a few last questions. Carrie stayed where she was, farther up the hallway, and watched as he graciously gave each reporter his attention.

Then he caught her in his peripheral vision. He glanced up and she smiled at him, and he did a double take. She could see him fighting a smile teasing at the corners of his mouth. The butterflies in her stomach flew into her throat. He listened to and answered the last question from the last reporter, and then he thanked them all, shook hands with his two hosts, and ushered everyone out of the hallway ahead of him. The hosts glanced her way as they passed her.

A wide smile broke out on his face as he neared her.

"David," she said. "You recognized me!"

"Of course! I'd know that smile anywhere. I can't believe you're here."

Until today it was a high school face Carrie had seen in her head, a high school voice she had heard. She couldn't have known what the grown-up face looked like, what the grown-up voice sounded like. And so she was surprised by both. The smooth, freckled visage she knew had a beard shadow now and lines around the eyes and mouth. The voice was a little different too—not so much deeper as throatier. Used. A fifty-year-old face. A fifty-year-old voice.

"Were you in there just now?" David asked.

"Yes."

"I didn't see you."

"You couldn't have in that throng."

He rolled his eyes. "I had no idea the press conference was going to turn into a spectacle."

"Well, you're a big deal. They can't believe their good fortune. They want everyone to know."

"I came here to work and be closer to family. I don't want to be put on display."

His fame hadn't gone to his head. He was still that guy.

"Don't worry, it'll die down."

"Not fast enough for me. They've got me doing a couple of interviews this afternoon!"

"I know. I'm one of them."

"What?"

"I'm your one o'clock. I'm doing a feature for *The Star*."

"You're a reporter?"

"I'm a freelance writer. I write all kinds of stuff for all kinds of publications. Not news usually, but in this case . . . ."

"You did it, then," said David. "You always knew you were going to be a writer."

"Just like you always knew you were going to be a doctor," Carrie replied.

"Have you lived here since your degree?"

"No, I worked in Vancouver for fifteen years."

He smiled knowingly at her. "But you came back home."

"Yup."

"We have a lot to catch up on." He pulled up his suit jacket sleeve and shirt cuff to look at his watch. "I'm afraid my first staff meeting starts in about fifteen minutes."

"Of course. I'll see you at 1 p.m." But instead of parting they stood awkwardly together for a moment. And Carrie was back standing on the step of her parents' house, making small talk with him, waiting for the goodnight kiss. They were so young and painfully shy it could keep them parting company for a half hour. Two teenagers whose only frame of reference was the movies. She'd wait for what seemed like an eternity for Rhett Butler to kiss Scarlett O'Hara, and then they'd both tilt the same way and their glasses would clash before their lips came even close.

"Must go," David said, averting his eyes. He touched her elbow. "It's so good to see you." And then he was gone.

Carrie took a deep breath and let it out. Had he been with her on that step just now?

...

Carrie was disappointed to find the CEO of the health region in David's office when she arrived for the interview. He was settled in a chair at David's table with a fresh cup of coffee, clearly expecting to be part of the interview, or at least to control it. David's raised eyebrows told her he hadn't expected it, either. Her plan to have a friendly conversation with David had to be abandoned. And so she put on her professional face and conducted the interview as such, and after the allotted hour had passed, she gave both men a business card and left.

Neither Carrie nor David had revealed to the CEO that they knew each other. Had David done so she might have concluded he thought of her only casually; she was just someone he knew long ago. As it was, her imagination was in overdrive as she walked to her car. A secret between them made their relationship special, personal.

Her phone rang as she was crossing the parking lot. It was David. "How about dinner tonight?" he said.

Her heart skipped a beat. "They haven't got something planned for you?" She had planned to call him in a week or so and ask *him* out for dinner, once he had settled in.

"No, they're doing it tomorrow night, after Annie arrives." David's wife. Tomorrow. She thought Annie wouldn't arrive for a few weeks, when the deal on the new house closed, according to a realtor friend of hers.

"I'd love to have dinner with you tonight," she said. Tonight could be her only chance. And she'd been planning what to say for months anyway, ever since she learned of his move back.

"How's Butler's, seven-thirty?" asked David.

"I'll meet you there!" replied Carrie.

"Looking forward to it. See you then."

The posh dining room on the top floor of The Hotel, downtown. That must be where they were putting him up. And by tomorrow night he'd be sharing his room with his wife. She had to take a deep breath to still her racing thoughts.

...

Carrie arrived for dinner a little late. She wanted David to be seated, let him decide what to do. After all, this wasn't an interview any more. Would he choose a friendly hug, maybe a kiss, even if only on the cheek? She followed the maître d' up a flight of stairs. She'd never been to Butler's before—it wasn't within her and her husband's reach—but she'd heard about it.

David rose from his chair as she approached.

"Hello there," he said as he pulled out her chair for her. Carrie said hello and breathed in his Old Spice aftershave as it wafted over her. He wasn't quite shaving when they dated in high school, but she recognized it; her dad used the same. A classic choice. David returned to his side of the table. No hug, no kiss, just polite.

Their last meeting more than twenty-five years ago had been the same. A chance encounter in an empty lecture theatre at the university. He sat easily and comfortably on an armrest in the row behind her seat, put a foot up on the seatback beside her, and leaned on the anatomy book he balanced on his knee. She had turned toward him and they chatted about their classes while she looked as meaningfully as possible into his eyes. Her powers of seduction weren't what she'd hoped. And she never ran into him again.

Their round table at Butler's was draped with white linen and set for two with glistening china and sparkling crystal. It sat next to a ceiling-to-floor window, and she looked out, admiring the view of the river. Carrie didn't want to look too eager by speaking first, and David seemed to be thinking the same thing. But a tuxedoed waiter arrived at the table and took the lead, letting them both off the hook. David asked her if she'd like an aperitif and at her positive response ordered a Dubonnet without hesitation. He was used to this life.

"You look great," Carrie said to him after the waiter walked away. A little clichéd but she couldn't help it. Same mane of dirty-blond hair but cut shorter now, a little grey at the temples. Same hazel eyes with their characteristic twinkle.

Same full lips.

"Thank you, so do you," David replied. Of course he'd have to say so but her heart soared anyway. Those months of dieting had paid off, and the little black dress had been well worth it.

And so it began. She asked him about his life as a heart surgeon and he asked her about hers as a writer. Friendly. Comfortable. No risk taking. Not like the night they sat in his parents' rec room, unbeknownst to his older brother upstairs, his parents in Europe. They drank vodka with orange juice until their heads swam and talked until 3 a.m. They were sixteen then and full of nerve. Life experience had made her more cautious now, but she'd been dreaming of this moment for more than thirty years. What did she have to lose?

But when their salads and then their beef Wellington arrived they turned to fine dining and a fabulous Cabernet, and they talked about high school and university and all the people they had known together. Procrastinating, avoiding anything too personal.

After their plates had been cleared, Carrie decided to go for it, her heart pounding inside her chest. After all, what did she have to lose? "I've thought about you a lot over the years," she said.

David's wineglass stopped on its way to his mouth. He looked at her. "Oh?" And then he took a drink.

Oh? Suddenly she *realized* what she had to lose—the fantasy. The one where he had wished all these years as much as she had that they had stayed together, maybe made a life together. Now she was back at the high school graduation dance and afterparty. Despite their breakup a few months earlier, David had been her escort. At the time she wondered if her best friend Eileen had something to do with his inviting her, but she was too happy to be with him again to care. She was hoping somehow he had forgiven her and they might get back together.

But it was not to be. Even though they had a great time together, he kept it friendly all evening, nothing more. She tried to make her feelings known without actually coming out and saying what she should have said—everything, in fact, that she was about to say now. But it was clear then that it was just one night for him. She had been disappointed and hurt, possibly as much as he had been those months earlier. She even wondered later if he was getting back at her. But that wasn't David.

She watched him now as he wiped his mouth with his napkin. "I wondered what might have happened if we'd stayed together," she said.

An odd silence. He was studying her face, furrows forming in his brow. Then he shrugged. "We were just kids." He paused, looked at the last swallow of Cabernet in his glass, swirled it around. "But I'm curious what went wrong. I thought we were getting along really well." He downed the last swallow of his wine.

Carrie's throat was suddenly dry. She had hurt him all those years ago, as she thought. Why otherwise would he be curious now? If it hadn't affected him, he would have easily brushed it off. She had hoped all these years that he assumed her parents wouldn't let her see him anymore after that night they were out until three o'clock in the morning, but she had been kidding herself.

She drank from her wineglass and swallowed hard. "Eileen told me you had been dating someone from another school while you were dating me."

His eyes widened. "What? I was *not!*" He looked unwaveringly into her eyes and she could see his anger. She knew he was telling the truth. "Why would you believe such a thing?"

"Eileen and I had been best friends since grade school. I trusted her."

"But why didn't you ask me if what she said about me was true?"

"I was angry . . . and hurt. But a couple of weeks after you and I broke up I realized the timing of her information was coincident with her boyfriend dumping her. I think she wanted me to be as miserable and alone as she was."

"She would do that to you?"

"She probably thought I would be spending all my time with *you*, and she had no other friends."

David scoffed. "I think I understand why."

The waiter returned with the dessert menu. He waited while she and David made a decision and then left them alone again.

"Still, I handled it badly, David. I should have known you well enough to know you couldn't possibly have been dating anyone else. I should have trusted *you*, not Eileen. If I hadn't reacted so quickly to what she had told me—"

"You still could have come to me, even a couple of weeks later."

"Well, then I was embarrassed and you wouldn't even look at me when I passed you in the hall or saw you in class. I thought you were really angry with me. Carrie's eyes started to prick with tears, "I'm so sorry." The waiter saved her again by arriving with crème caramel and coffee.

David sat back in his chair and seemed to study, for an eternity, the dessert spoon he held between his thumb and forefinger. Then he looked up and drew her eyes to his. "And you've been carrying this around with you all these years?"

"I have never forgiven myself."

"But *I* had forgiven you. I asked you to grad, hoping you were not still angry with me, even though I didn't know the reason you were. I was hoping we might get back together."

"What? That's what I was hoping too! But you didn't even kiss me that night or call me afterward."

David put down his dessert spoon and leaned toward her. "Eileen stopped me in the hall one day at school, after I had asked you to grad, and told me you had started dating someone else, but he was older, from university, so he didn't want to go to a high school grad. She said that's why you said yes to my invitation. But at that point I wouldn't pull out on you."

Carrie sat back and rubbed her temples with

her fingers. "I can't believe it," she said, "she got us both."

"Yes, she did. And not only that. I did the same thing you did: I didn't ask you if it was true." They stared at each other for a few seconds, their heads shaking in disbelief. They picked up their spoons and started in on their dessert. There wasn't anything more they could say.

And then there was music coming from the other side of the room, something jazzy and slow. Carrie hadn't even noticed the stage and its piano there, nor the quartet arriving. David put down his spoon, stood, and held out his hand to her. And they walked to the gleaming wood floor in front of the stage. And when he took her into his arms, it really was like in the movies. She had been imagining his touch for thirty years. He laid his cheek against her forehead and they held each other, knowing nothing would come of it, knowing neither of them would hurt their spouses, knowing it was too late.

...

Carrie felt a hand from behind on her left shoulder. "You're not sleeping," said her husband.

"Just a little wired, I guess," she replied.

"How was he?"

"Good. He was good."

Her husband tucked in close and laid his arm across her waist.

And she laced her fingers into his.

The Plan

"I'll always have a dog!" he growled.

Right on cue.

"Well, if that's how you feel, I guess we'll be parting company," Fran replied. His eyes widened for a split second. He wasn't ready for that. He couldn't find the word immediately, but she knew what it would be. She watched the vein on his forehead fill with angry blood and waited for it, her heart racing.

"Fine!"

There it was.

He brushed past her and pounded down the hallway, grabbing his keys off the hall table on the way. The door to the garage opened and then slammed shut. As she walked into the den she could hear the overhead door roll up. She watched through the window as his truck backed out onto the street. It skidded a bit on the asphalt as he hit the gas. He ignored the stop sign at the top of the cul de sac and screeched up the street.

Fran sat down at the desk, her hands shaking. It had gone just as she expected, as she wanted it to, but that didn't make it any easier. Even after thirty-five years, it hurt to be so disrespected. But it was the last time. She needed to focus on the plan, what she needed to do next, not think about him anymore.

It wasn't really about a dog, of course. It would be silly to end a marriage over a dog. Besides, she loved dogs. But when, three months earlier, Dandy could no longer get up without help, his poor old hips, she realized that life without a dog was just around the corner, and suddenly life without a husband seemed possible too. She could never leave a dog with him, but she could leave if there was no dog. It was an opportunity she'd never had before. There was always a dog, and then there was always a second dog when the first one got old.

Until Dandy. She'd put her foot down about a second dog. He didn't like it, but he didn't want to do all the work of the new dog, either, which she threatened to foist upon him. And so he relented. And suddenly there was hope. Hope for a new life—a life of her own making. She'd immediately begun preparing.

Fran had known that facing her husband with something abstract, like unhappiness, would lead to the usual to and fro, with the same inevitable result—anger on his side, heartache on hers—and her spirit just wasn't up to it. She'd been nurturing it the last few months, but she knew it to be as tattered as an old flag in a high wind. She had to make it easy on herself. But she refused to slink quietly away, and so she had decided to focus on the new-dog issue, not get personal. She would say no to a new dog. She would not give in to him, not this time, and he certainly wouldn't concede to her, of that she could be sure. So that would be it. Simple as that. It would be the last time he would not listen to her, the last time he would dismiss her feelings so quickly and casually that she wondered if she had even spoken them aloud.

Dandy had been gone a few weeks now, so she knew it wouldn't be long. The question of getting a new dog was bound to come up. She knew what his reaction to her would be. You can't be with a man for that many years and not know him. The very *idea* of her saying no to him, as if she had the power to do so, would enrage him. And it did. He wouldn't hurt her, at least not physically. He wasn't that type. He preferred to show Fran her place, let her know how wrong she was, how powerless. But it didn't matter what he said, not this time.

Still, she was nervous. She had never lived alone, never managed her own life. She had no idea what it would be like. That was the scariest part—the unknown. It was what had kept her with him all these years. She always thought the known was better than the unknown. But time was running out. The known was not better anymore. Happiness was better. True happiness. The kind inside you.

He would be gone a few hours, determined to show her how mad he was, and then he would calm down, get home in time for supper. In the meantime she had things to do. And she could revel in her new-found power and the shock and disbelief she had seen on his face, even the devastation he might feel later. Revenge was never good motivation for any action, but she would allow herself a little of its sweetness for now. She needed the calories for the strength she would require to recreate herself, her life.

She took a deep, mind-clearing breath, sat tall in the desk chair in the den, and clicked on her to-do list, typing in "happiness," when it prompted her for her password. This list was her last, the others taken care of as Dandy's health had worsened.

She clicked on "print," grabbed her red pen out of the box in the middle desk drawer, and checked off the tasks laid out on the page as she completed them. After her two suitcases and few boxes were in the trunk of her car, she did a last walk around the house, making sure she hadn't forgotten anything. She needn't have. After months of preparation and planning, she knew she had everything that was important. Her husband hadn't noticed things gone from closets and drawers. He might now notice that the dog pictures were gone off the wall in the den, but not right away, as he rarely went in there. It would be too late anyway.

She would miss her house and all of her things in it, for a while, but she expected to see at least some of it again in the divorce settlement. If she didn't, so be it. It would be disappointing, after all the time, money, and energy spent making their house a home, but not earth-shattering. Besides, it might be nice to start over in every way, everything new.

Fran glanced at her watch; an hour had passed since he left the house. She was right on time. She went to the hall table for her purse, then headed into the garage and locked the door behind her.

She pressed the button to open the big overhead door and got into her car. She slid the key into the ignition and turned the car on, fastened her seatbelt, then looked into the rear-view mirror.

And her mouth fell open.

She watched in horror as her husband's truck loomed large behind her car and then disappeared from her view as it pulled into the garage on her passenger side. Her mouth went dry. Why was he back so quickly? She thought she'd have lots of time, be long gone before he returned home. This wasn't like him. She gripped the steering wheel to steady herself, crescent moons of white popping out on her knuckles.

She didn't look over at him as he parked, keeping her eyes on the storage cabinet in front of her car. She waited for him to get out of the truck, to ensure he didn't open his door and hit her side mirror just as she was backing out. She could see him in her peripheral vision, waited for him to go directly to the door of the house, ignore her, assume incorrectly she was just going to do errands. Never imagine she was leaving for good.

But he didn't. He didn't go to the door. He was tapping on her passenger window. She didn't want to respond, didn't want to look at him.

Didn't want to be sidetracked, her plan interrupted. Why wasn't he going to the door? She could hear him saying her name, trying to get her attention.

Fran slowly turned her head.

He was bent over, looking in, motioning for her to lower the window. His body blocked the light from the overhead doorway to his face. She hadn't prepared for this. Why? Why hadn't she thought of this? He had never returned this quickly before, that's why. Never. She pressed the button in the armrest at her left until she knew the window was partly, but not all the way, open. Her eyes returned to the cabinet. He said her name, tried to get her to look at him, but she didn't move.

"I'm sorry, dear," he said.

She renewed her grip on the wheel. She didn't want his apology.

"I thought about it, and you're right." He paused. "We shouldn't get another dog right away."

She didn't respond.

"You're going shopping?" A pause. "Well, have fun. See you when you get back." Another pause.

And then he rose to a standing position and

walked to the door. Fran could hear his keys jangling as he looked for the right one. She didn't want to look at him. He was virtually in her line of sight and she resisted. But then he turned back to look at her, and the motion drew her eyes.

And her breath caught.

His face was red and his eyes bloodshot and wet. Even at the distance she was from him, she could see it. In thirty-five years she had never seen him cry, not even when the dogs died. Crying? She couldn't believe it. And then he smiled weakly at her and said "I love you." Not loudly—he wouldn't want the neighbours to hear—but she definitely heard it through the open window, saw it in the movement of his lips. And then he turned back to the door, unlocked and opened it, and disappeared into the house.

No, No, NO!

Fran slammed both palms against the steering wheel. Don't give in to it! Don't do it! It doesn't mean a thing! But she could feel her resolve crumbling. He had been *crying*. He had been upset, maybe thinking about Dandy. She blinked frantically as tears welled in her eyes, and she grabbed a tissue from the box beside her. Maybe he did have a heart, after all. But then her eyes were drawn to her list and the red pen sitting on the seat, three items still unchecked.

And she dabbed the tears from her eyes.

And smiled.

She backed out of the garage, lowering the driver's window all the way down. She pressed the button on the remote control to lower the overhead door and, before she reached the pavement on the cul de sac, she threw the remote control out the window and into the bushes lining the driveway. As she backed onto the street she put a red checkmark next to "leave the remote." She pulled up to the stop sign at the top of the cul de sac and pressed redial on her cell phone. She could hear the excited yips of playing puppies when the call was picked up.

"Is Dandie ready?" she asked.

"She's all ready to go," replied the woman on the other end.

"I'll be there in twenty minutes."

"Okay! I'll take her out for one last pee. She's been playing hard with her brothers and sisters, so she should sleep well in the car."

"That's great—I can't wait to see her!" Fran turned her phone off and checked off "call the breeder" on her list.

And then she flicked her signal light on and, with a flourish befitting the occasion, put a large checkmark through the last item, "STICK TO THE PLAN!" and drove away.

A Man and His Camel

Brenda paused at the top of the neighbourhood ravine, thinking again about her decision to walk the dog in it today. It was draped in a sodden white blanket of snow, and the branches of the Douglas firs hung low under its weight. The snow was still coming down, but the soft, quiet flakes of early morning were now tiny pellets bouncing noisily off her nylon jacket. The asphalt path descending from the street into the ravine had turned to smokey-grey glass gnarled with footprints—human and dog—only partly frozen in the near-melting temperature.

She knew she should stay up on the street, where city snowplows were working overnight, but managing Jackson on leash wasn't easy. Jerry always handled him before, and she and the dog were still adjusting to their new arrangement together. For now, this was the best place to bring him; here she could let him run off leash.

She longed to leave winter behind. When Jerry was alive she could pick and choose the days she accompanied him and Jackson on their walk—dry, sunny ones that lifted her spirit and warmed her heart. Soggy, grey ones rounded her body and slowed her mind. But dogs didn't care about the weather, and she had promised Jerry she would take good care of his dog.

Brenda looked up at the sky. It was only mid-morning, but there appeared little hope the sun would make an appearance. She took a deep breath and started down the path. She considered the less precarious route along the sides of the treacherous ice, but concluded that slogging through moisture-heavy, knee-deep snow would be no less difficult. She placed her feet carefully, wary of the frozen layers beneath the slushy surface. She missed her husband's strong hand in hers. She was consoled only by the fact that if the forecast was correct, in a day or two this would be nothing but a dirty river dotted with icy islands of boot treads and paw pads. After all, it was the end of April.

Jackson was not deterred by the conditions. Once off leash, he left the path and waded through the snow, hip deep, leaping jackrabbit style in an attempt to make better ground, occasionally diving beneath the surface to scoop the wet white stuff into his mouth. At times she could hardly see him. If it wasn't for his Dalmatian spots he would disappear altogether.

Brenda was breathing hard, slipping and catching herself. She could feel the sweat running down the middle of her back. And now her face was flushed with heat, no doubt a glorious, volcanic red. She cursed aloud. It was foolish to come here today. She stopped to catch her breath and rummaged through her jacket pocket for a tissue.

And then she saw a man coming around a stand of blue spruce far below, climbing the path toward her. A chocolate Labrador retriever forged ahead of him, crisscrossing the path as dogs do, not wanting to miss anything along the way.

Her stomach clenched. She was a woman alone and in a place well hidden by trees. She never had to worry about this sort of thing when Jerry was alive. She looked back up the path, but the distance back to the street was greater than the distance between her and the man, and it was clear that the ice and snow were not slowing him down in the least. He would catch up to her before she got far.

Jackson reached the strangers first, and after the requisite identification ritual the two dogs began to box like kangaroos, then broke away and plowed through the snow, spots in pursuit of chocolate. Brenda was somewhat relieved. If the dog was friendly, chances were the owner was, too. She stuffed the soggy tissue back into her pocket and carried on down the path, focused only on getting past the man as quickly as possible. She locked her eyes onto her feet and tried to look determined.

"Hello," said the stranger as they were almost upon each other, and she jumped, startled by his voice.

"Hello," she replied, hoping he didn't detect her nervousness. He stopped, so she stopped too, like two dog walkers would if their dogs were playing.

Despite the snow still coming down, the man wore nothing on his head. He was clean shaven and his dirty-blond hair was drawn tightly back in a ponytail. Brenda's heart fluttered a little. Jerry wore a ponytail when she first met him, and she fell hard for him. This man was thirty years old, at most, and that made him more than twenty years her junior. Suddenly she was aware of how bad she must look. Her woolen toque only drew attention to her face, which was without makeup until she showered after Jackson's walk, and her nose was dripping again with the exertion of her descent farther into the ravine. She quickly turned her attention to the dogs running in and out of the trees and dabbed her nose as discreetly as she could with the back of her glove.

"Kind o' Christmassy out here," she said as she stole another glance at him. He was watching the dogs, too. Just two dog walkers doing what dog walkers do. The corner of her mouth twitched.

"Sure is," he replied. His voice was smooth, like liquid honey.

"It's beautiful, really, but not quite what I had in mind for April."

"It's not surprising for April, though."

She nodded in agreement. "What's your dog's name?"

"Mr. Jingles."

She turned to him. "Like the mouse in that movie *The Green Mile*?" He turned to her and she looked into stunning blue eyes, almost turquoise, like the water she and Jerry saw in the Caribbean years ago.

"No. Like my camel."

She smiled at him, conscious of every line she knew just formed on her face, hoping that her morning cereal wasn't stuck in her teeth. "Your camel?"

He smiled back, showing perfectly aligned pearly whites. "Yeah, my camel's name was Mr. Jingles."

"You had a camel?"

"Well, he wasn't really mine, but after spending three hundred days with him we were really close."

"Three hundred days? You're one of those . . . those guys that . . . that . . . went across the . . . the . . . ." She sounded like an idiot.

"The Empty Quarter."

"That's right! I didn't recognize you." How could she? The television clips of the expedition showed heavily bearded and robed men, filthy and sweaty. She couldn't have appreciated the strong jaw line on this one. The Greek nose.

"No," he said.

"No, what?"

"That wasn't me."

"It wasn't?"

"No."

"Well, you've got me, then. What about the camel?" She was sure it would be an equally fabulous story.

"I took care of him at the zoo a while back. Now he's in Japan, in the Kyoto Zoo."

"How interesting," she said, showing her age. She groaned inside. "And you named your dog after him." He nodded, but that I've-got-to-get-going expression had appeared on his face. She'd lost him.

Jackson saved the day and came roaring to Brenda with Mr. Jingles on his tail. He slammed on his brakes on the slippery path, but it was too late, and he hit her squarely in the knees. Mr. Jingles bowled both Jackson and her over, and they, all three, fell in a heap into the deep snow beside the path. The two dogs clambered to their feet and stood over her, licking her face, and she giggled like the girl she used to be.

"Are you okay?" asked Mr. Jingles' walker as he removed his glove and extended her a hand up.

"Yeah, it was a soft landing," replied Brenda. She declined his help, but noticed the slender fingers and manicured nails. "It feels kinda good down here. I think I'll stay a minute." She didn't tell him she needed to wait for the pain in her knees to subside.

He looked at her like she'd lost her mind. He said, "See ya, then," and she said, "See ya. Nice talkin' to you," and she watched his behind as he continued on up the path with Mr. Jingles. Grinning like the infamous Cheshire cat, she closed her eyes to hold the memory in as the snow pellets cooled her hot face.

A moment later, Jackson yawned noisily to get her attention. She opened her eyes to find him standing over her, and the smell of wet dog assailed her nostrils. She tousled the top of his head and sent him off to find a stick. He jackrabbited to the nearest tree, where he ducked under the drooping branches and disappeared.

The snow stopped suddenly. Brenda watched the sun slip into a sliver of blue sky and she smiled.

And then she made an angel in the snow.